TEACH HER

FORBIDDEN FANTASIES: A FEMALE PROFESSOR/MALE STUDENT ROMANCE

ANGEL DEVLIN

ALL RIGHTS RESERVED.
No part of this publication may be reproduced, distributed, or transmitted in any form or by any means, including photocopying, recording, or other electronic or mechanical methods, without the prior written permission of the publisher, with the exception of the use of small quotations in book reviews.
Copyright © 2017 by Angel Devlin.
Second edition, © 2022 by Angel Devlin
Book cover design by The Pretty Little Design Company.
Formatting by Angel Devlin.

This is a work of fiction. Any resemblance of characters to actual persons, living or dead, is purely coincidental. Angel Devlin holds exclusive rights to this work. Unauthorized duplication is prohibited.

CHAPTER ONE

Meredith

Being a professor got really stressful at times and that was why sometimes, if we stayed late preparing lesson plans or marking, myself and Marcus Wilson would give each other a helping hand to release some of the tension. We weren't fuck buddies—it had never gone that far—we were come buddies.

It had begun the middle of last year. A day that had been extraordinarily hot, and I had had fractious and short-tempered students being smart asses the whole day. It was a problem I expected to address only at the beginning of a semester. The grad students were at least eighteen years old, and at twenty-five I wasn't *that* much their senior. But senior I was, and I had made sure they had learned that pretty damn quick. For the most part students were respectful, but you always had the odd one who had had a bad day or was struggling with life at that particular time. The day we became come buddies, a student had walked out of class after giving me a heap of abuse and I was still new to that kinda confrontation. The stress, added to a shitload of work I had to finish and prepare, meant I had ended up in my office determined that I was not getting behind the wheel until I had calmed myself the fuck down. Marcus had also stayed late and popped in to my office to see me, before he left. We had gotten along pretty well from the get-go and maybe I would have dated him if either I had a) wanted a relationship, or b) it hadn't been against the college's policies. He was cute in an Orlando Bloom kind of way: sexy, but with a young and fresh face, freckles, and a smile that quirked the corner of his lip.

"You look like you need vodka," he'd told me, taking a hip flask from his laptop bag and handing it over.

"That transparent, huh?" I'd replied. "I've been in here for two hours now, trying to get caught up on things and attempting to calm myself down."

He'd lightly stroked my forearm. "I heard about the face-off with Fleishman."

A heavy sigh had left my mouth. "I'm trying to forget about it."

He beckoned me upright and put an arm around me. "Come here. Let Prof. Wilson give you one of his amazing hugs."

Despite the heat, I'd snuggled up into his arms. It had been exactly what I'd needed. Just to know that someone else gave a damn that my day had been the pits. However, after a few minutes it was clear that we were both too hot.

"Thanks, but I am going to pass out if I stay next to your shirt any longer." I smiled.

"Well, I could always take it off?" he'd said.

"I don't want a relationship."

"Neither do I. Why don't we just give each other a helping hand... or tongue." He'd winked. "Get rid of some of that stress."

The day had sucked and so I'd thought fuck it. I'd not dated anyone for over a year due to a bad break up and the thought of enjoying myself with no baggage had sounded fine to me.

So that's when it had started—*the helping hand.*

We'd ended up back here today. Back in my office on the very last day of term. Marcus was leaving. Everyone had gone, and it was just the two of us.

"So, what do you think?" he said to me, "Go big, or go home?"

I unbuttoned my blouse, revealing the white lacy bra I wore underneath.

"Well, it's you, so I would say it's most definitely go big."

Marcus had a nine-inch cock. It was larger than any cock I'd ever seen before. I'd become practiced in the art of jacking him off with my hands and my mouth, but today—our very last time together—we were going for the grand finale, and I couldn't wait. It had been so long since I'd ridden any cock, never mind one that I fully expected to give me a good time. Plus, the thought of someone walking in on us since we'd started doing this, made my juices flow. Now we were going to fuck, I was in danger of flooding the college.

Marcus stripped out of all his clothes and then grabbed me and pushed me over to the wall. Kneeling at my feet, he pulled my thong down my thighs, calves, and off, leaving them bunched at the side of him, then he moved my thighs apart. My pussy was swollen and ready to accept the tongue that knew exactly how to bring me off. His mouth fastened on my bud sucking eagerly and he pushed two fingers inside my soaking wet heat.

"Oh my god. Yes."

Within a minute I had to hold his head with my hands as I tried to push my core closer to his mouth. My cream dripped down his face as I exploded against his lips.

We paused for a moment as he allowed me the time to recover from my shudders.

Changing position, I took him in my mouth. I was still so horny my juices ran down my legs and dripped onto the floor. Marcus groaned as I sucked him right to the back of my throat, but because this time things were to end differently, I kept stopping when I felt him get too eager, so he didn't come in my mouth.

"Ready?" he asked me.

"Yes."

He unwrapped a condom and placed it on his cock and then he lined himself up with my entrance, pushing in deep. I could feel his girth slowly sinking inside my walls, filling me up inch by glorious inch and I couldn't help but make noises. I loved to talk dirty too.

"Oh fuck. Why didn't we do this sooner? Oh my, your cock is so huge. It's filling me right up."

Marcus' hands gripped my hips harder. He didn't

speak. Instead, he showed me with his actions that he was enjoying himself.

As I began to raise my hips to meet his thrusts, he moved his hands around to my breasts, leaning down to capture a nipple in his mouth which he then sucked on.

"Ooooooohhhh."

I felt myself building towards completion once more. Marcus abandoned my nipple as he concentrated more on the rhythm of his thrusts. Though he quickened his pace, he remained quite gentle though and to be honest I wanted him to fuck me hard, so I told him so.

He thrust a little harder, but I could tell it wasn't his thing and he returned to giving me a slow and steady fucking. I needed more and so while he thrust inside me, I reached down and played with my own clit until I felt the tremors of my come begin. I quivered around his cock, milking it as he reached his own climax with an, "Oh God," of his own. He pulled me in close to him and we stayed there, joined together, bodies close until we got our breath back. Then he looked up at me.

"Goodbye, Prof. Butler. It's been a pleasure."

"It certainly has." I peeled myself away from his body and I picked up my panties. "What am I going to do for stress relief now?" I laughed, as we cleaned ourselves up with our discarded underwear.

"Looks like you'll have to discover wine."

He knew I didn't drink much though he didn't know why.

"Maybe."

"It's a shame I'm moving so far away," he said. "We could still have met up."

"I'll have to bring a battery-operated boyfriend with me to college along with my laptop." I winked. "And seeing as I have one that looks exactly like a lipstick, I'll have to make sure not to reapply in front of the students, just in case I take out the wrong one."

He laughed. "So, what are you doing over the break then? You know I'm relocating. What are your plans?"

"I'm going to hit the gym hard," I said. "I've wimped out so many times after classes because of being exhausted. It's time to get my fitness back up to its prior levels. Other than that, not a lot. I intend to visit my family for as short a time as I can get away with and hit the beach to get a golden glow."

He leaned over and kissed my cheek.

"No. We can't leave it like that," I told him and I placed my hands at the back of his head and brought his lips to mine. We had never kissed on the mouth. Intimate kisses of private areas but never our mouths. The kiss was long, tender, and a proper goodbye.

He left. I watched him go and then I sat back on my chair for a while, so that we didn't leave together. It was something Marcus had always insisted on. I didn't give a damn if the janitor saw us walk out together. They could assume what they liked, there was no proof. We kept the door locked. Next semester wouldn't be the same.

Try as I might though, I couldn't conjure up any real feelings for Marcus. He really had been a means to an end. Like a real-life dildo. I felt guilty about my feelings, but it was for the best that while I had enjoyed our make-outs, I had developed nothing in the way of a crush and had never wanted to take it further. He was now gone and my sex life had left with him, but if I missed anything, it would be our friendship.

I had indeed gotten myself back to the gym. My body had toned enough that I felt happy wearing my tiniest gym shorts and a crop top. My arms and thighs were well defined now, and my abs had a six pack I was immensely proud of. I made a promise to myself that no matter how stressful college got when I returned, I would maintain a fitness regime to keep myself toned. Maybe I wouldn't be able to maintain the athletic figure I had right now, but I felt so much better in myself when I was fitter, and so the gym and the pool needed to become part of my own curriculum. I was so busy daydreaming, I stumbled on the treadmill and felt myself falling, only to be caught by a well-toned pair of arms.

"Fuck. Thanks so much," I told the owner of them as I rubbed the back of my neck. "I let my concentration go. Stupid of me. I think that's a sign I need to stop and get some water."

"Stand there. I'll get you a drink," the guy said, and I watched as he walked away.

He was of medium build, around six feet tall, and had almost jet-black hair that was a little grown out. I guessed you'd call it shaggy. His eyes had been the most piercing blue, and chiseled cheekbones and a full pout made him look like some kind of model. I guessed that's exactly what he was, plenty of models frequented my gym. They sold photos to independent authors to use as their cover pictures on books; and our gym owner, Macy, an obsessive reader, liked to frame the covers and put them up on walls around the gym. Hell, I had no objections! It was better than staring at my own sweaty body while I exercised. I'd chatted to a few of the models at times. Some were lovely and down to earth, while others thought they were God's gift to men and women, but I'd never seen this guy before so I presumed he was a new one.

He walked back over and held out the drink to me. I stared at him a little more while trying not to be too obvious about it.

"Thanks," I said as I reached for the paper cup of water. I drank it down greedily.

"Nice tat," he said to me when I'd finished and could speak again. He nodded toward my upper hip. Visible above my gym shorts was a tattoo of an egg timer, the sand was part pouring out. The timer was black and the sand purple and aqua blue. It was only small, but I'd had it done at the beginning of the summer break to remind me that life carried on whether I was being present in my life or not. I'd done a lot of thinking and looking inward during vacation time and had vowed to open myself up to new opportunities. I'd been scared to get into another relationship, having found the heartbreak of before so soul destroying, but Marcus had helped me see that I wanted more. Maybe not a relationship still—I remained cautious after my break-up with Chad—but I wanted my heart to thump faster and I liked things on the dirtier side of the spectrum. I'd wanted Marcus to pound me hard on our onetime fuck. As a full-on lover, he wouldn't have been enough. I also liked the danger that we could have been caught. I wondered how people found lovers who could give them what they wanted and whether it just came from a relationship developing over time. My big break-up relationship had contained perfectly adequate sex, but we were both new to relationships. Chad and I had met at high school and neither of us had been confident enough to ask for what we wanted. Still, I'd loved Chad, and it had killed me inside when we'd broken up after six years together.

"Perhaps I would have been better grabbing you an espresso?" the guy stated, and I realized I had completely zoned out on him.

"Jeez, I'm so sorry. I really don't feel quite myself today." I looked down at my tat. "It's there to remind me that life is short and to enjoy myself," I explained.

"I wholeheartedly agree," he replied. "But today I think you should call it a day and head home and grab some sleep. Start the whole 'making the most of life' mantra tomorrow."

I laughed. "Yes, you're right. I'm going to get showered under very cold water, grab a coffee—though I'll make it a latte rather than espresso—and then I'm gonna head on home to sunbathe on the deck in the shade, where I may just fall asleep. Thank you once again for coming to my rescue." I held up my empty paper cup. "And for the water."

"No problem," he replied. Those blue eyes twinkled when he smiled and revealed perfect, white teeth. He held out a hand. "Garrett."

"I'm Meredith." I decided to brazen it out. "Are you one of the cover models?"

He shook his head and laughed. "No. I'm nothing special. Just here to make the most of what God gave me and keep it healthy, you know?"

"Totally. My summer has been devoted to it. Well, that and catching up on trash TV, but I don't usually admit to that. Anyway, enough of my chatting. I ramble on when I first meet someone, I think it's nerves. See you around." I said, and then I left, moving as quickly as I could. I felt rather stupid that I'd asked if he was a model now. He probably thought I was some kind of groupie, jeez. That would not do. I would have to work on potential topics of conversation that didn't make me out to be some complete brainless airhead. What was it I had said? That I wanted to catch up on reality TV. Dear God. The guy had looked a little younger than me and yet he had seemed so much more mature in the confidence that had oozed from him and how he had handled himself. I seriously could do with some pointers. Maybe for now though I would just change the time I went to the gym slightly, so I could avoid embarrassing myself again for the last week of the break.

CHAPTER TWO

Meredith

The rest of the break passed far too quickly. I lived in a small studio apartment in Brooklyn, where I'd taken over the tenancy from a high school teacher called Parker just after college was out for the summer. He had been giving up teaching he'd told me; instead he would work for his father's publishing company. He was also getting married. I had to admit I had experienced feelings of jealousy that he and his fiancée were buying a large new home while I was taking over their old, small apartment, but it was within my budget from my professor's salary and I was thankful I had seen the rental ad almost the minute it had appeared on a teaching forum I belonged to on the internet for all teachers and professors in the New York vicinity.

There was room in the corner for a queen bed. In another corner there was a small kitchenette, and nearby room for a small dining table and chairs. That was the set-up Parker had had. There was a separate bathroom off to the rear. I had brought my queen bed from the old apartment I had shared with Tana, a fellow professor at college. She had fallen in love and gotten married, so I had needed to find myself somewhere else to live. I'd had enough of sharing my space. I wanted a place of my own. One where I did not have to hear an engaged couple having noisy sex almost every night. Where Parker had had his table and chairs, I put a desk. I could eat with my plate balanced on my lap, but also there was a small piece of countertop in the kitchen area that I could buy a stool for. I wanted somewhere to do my work, so the desk won.

At the opposite side of the room to my bed I had a small black couch and a large floor lamp and a television mounted on the wall that could be swiveled to face either the couch or the bed. The place was tiny, but I'd done my best to make it my own.

I got my bag ready with what I needed for work and placed the clothes I planned to wear over the back of the bathroom door. After eating and then reading for a while, I settled down under the comforter to get a good night's sleep. I'd enjoyed the break but now it was back to early starts.

My new students had seemed okay. This year I was teaching about tax. Not the most interesting of subjects for the majority of people, but I loved math and accounting. It had been strange not seeing Marcus' face when I had arrived, but I discovered he'd left me an envelope in my staff room locker which had said 'open at the end of the first day.' I sat in my office intrigued about what I would find. I tore open the envelope and extracted the typed letter.

Mer,

Are you missing me already? Hope you scored over the break or by now you'll no doubt be very stressed and are now without your helping hand. What are you gonna do?

Well, I have a dare for you if you are up to the challenge.

Unknown to most Profs and students in this college there's a secret group that gets together at the beginning of the new

semester to initiate any potential new roommates.

There was a drawing of a house and an arrow showing me where the 'Dares Room' was that the initiations took place in.

If you get the chance, dress down in black and sneak around there and look through the blinds. It will give you some naughty visuals to keep you occupied during any lonely nights or for when you need to reapply that 'lipstick' after college ;)

The final dare always takes place at 11pm on the first Friday so you have plenty of time to think it over and prepare. Just remember, you like the thought of being caught!

Enjoy!
Marcus.

I folded the letter and placed it in my purse. A kind of fraternity, here? At this small business college? I wondered how Marcus had gotten to know about it. The house he had drawn me a map of was on campus and not far from the student residences. I had always just assumed that it was rented out to a group of the wealthier students. And what had Marcus meant by naughty visuals? What the hell was the initiation about? He'd been a good guy, so I doubted what went on there was anything illegal. He'd been right though. The thought of watching some kind of daring initiation through the blind was a turn on. But wouldn't it be young students? I pulled a face. Depending on who it was it could be the complete opposite of sexy.

I gathered my belongings and headed straight to the gym. I was in a quandary. Did I do Marcus' dare for the sheer exhilaration of hiding around campus and the house and not being caught? I could always walk away if it was debauched, maybe even tell someone in a higher authority what was going on. That was it, I decided. I'd check it out because it might just be that I'd be doing people a favor if this needed to be made public and stopped. Worst case scenario I had to become a whistleblower, best case I had some fun.

Due to my extreme lack of any kind of social life, I'd decided to head to the gym every single night after college. I missed Tana. Though she'd been engaged, she'd still been my roomie, and we'd had a lot of laughs. It would take some time to get used to my own company. I liked living on my own, but it would be good to have some other friends to hang with occasionally. For now, I would have to put up with idle chatter at the gym with people whose names I never got to know or I failed to remember.

I walked into the gym and there he was—Garrett. I hadn't seen him since I'd fallen off the treadmill and embarrassed myself, having avoided him by attending at different times. It looked as if he too, had now changed the time he attended. As if he detected I was watching him his gaze met mine. He raised a hand in recognition and then returned to bench pressing. Relieved he wasn't heading over to me, I moved toward a treadmill.

After running for thirty minutes while listening to some tracks via my earbuds, I looked around to see if Garrett was still there. I'd been focused on my routine and had been stopping myself from thinking about either Garrett or the secret society. I didn't even know what my problem was with Garrett, anyway. Was I too scared to even talk to a guy now? Yes, my last break up had been nasty, but I couldn't stop myself from talking to men. One day I wanted marriage and a family. I wouldn't get them if I never talked to another man, would I? Having spotted Garrett on a rowing machine, I grabbed a paper cup of water for myself and one for him and I walked over to where he rowed.

"Hey there," I said. It wasn't the most exciting of conversation starters but at least I'd tried.

He stopped rowing, and I offered him one of the cups of water.

"Thanks. Hold it a minute," he requested, then he got up and dried himself on his nearby towel.

"I'd just been thinking I needed a drink," he said. "Though it wasn't water I'd been considering."

Before I could think the words, they were out of my mouth, "Well, we could always grab a couple beers?"

Garrett smiled. "And there I thought you'd been avoiding bumping into me again. Yet now here you are asking me on a date. Shows what I know about women." He laughed and once again his blue eyes twinkled.

I felt heat hit my cheeks. "I-it's not a date. I just needed to eat and so when you said—"

He put a hand out and touched my arm. "I'm messing with you. I need to eat too, so why don't we hit the showers and I'll meet you in the cafeteria afterward?"

He noticed my expression straightaway. "I only meant we would meet there, not eat there. See you in fifteen?"

I nodded and went off to the showers.

I was glad of the cool water to calm down the heat

that had hit my body with my embarrassment. Also, when he had said for us to hit the showers, it had brought to mind a vision of me pushed up against the wall, water pouring down my body, while those plump lips of his pressed against my own. It would appear I had developed a crush on Garrett the gym guy.

Whereas my usual MO was to shower and run. This time I showered, blew out my blonde, medium-length hair and put on a little makeup. I still managed to be out of the room within fifteen minutes though. As I headed toward the cafeteria, I could see Garrett was already waiting outside. He was talking to another guy, and I watched him, taking in that heavenly looking body and those chiseled features. Had I really scored a kinda date with this guy?

Garrett suggested a restaurant within walking distance of the gym that he said he'd been to a couple times before. I was happy with his suggestion and we ordered beer and some pasta. I found him real easy to chat to. He exuded confidence and kept our conversation light but continuous.

"So, what do you do for a living?" he asked me.

"I'm a professor in accountancy at King's Business College."

He almost choked on his drink.

"Excuse me?"

I repeated what I had said, then added, "What's so weird about that?"

He recovered himself and then spoke. "You just don't look much like an accounts professor. I guess I'm being stereotypical, but I would have expected a guy in his early fifties with spectacles."

"Yep. Stereotyping much? I happen to love figures," I told him.

"Me too," he quipped, following it up with a wink, "but somehow, I don't think we're talking about the same thing."

I smiled, but I felt my cheeks pink up, so I took a drink of my beer.

"If you don't find this question too personal, how old are you anyway?" he asked me.

"Hmmm, I don't know if it's right to ask a woman her age," I teased before admitting I was twenty-five. "How about you and what do you do?"

"Twenty-three," he replied, "and I'm a PT."

"Ah, sounds good," I told him. "Maybe I'll hire you to help me keep this body, because college is the worst for making me head straight home to pizza and wine."

He took a piece of paper and a pen from his duffle bag and wrote out a cell number. "Here you go. I am out of business cards right now, so this will have to do. If you want to tone up, call me. I'm sure we can arrange a gym-buddy discount for my new friend."

"That would be great," I said honestly. "I will give it some serious thought."

We'd finished our meals, and I was just drinking up the last of my beer when Garrett raised the subject of relationships. Damn. Another five minutes and I could have been out of there unscathed.

"I haven't dated for a long while," I told him, deciding to be honest. "Without going into too many details, I had a long-term relationship which ended badly. My ex developed a drink problem. He got abusive."

"He ever hit you?" Garrett's jaw had tightened.

"No. I didn't let it get that far. He grabbed me once and got in my face. It was scary enough for me. I left him and moved back in with my parents for a short while until I rented an apartment with a friend."

"Guys like that make my blood boil," he answered.

"Yeah, well, it was a long time ago now."

"Not long enough if you are still wary of dating," he replied.

I shrugged my shoulders. "I came out with you for a drink, didn't I? So I'm getting back out there. Though this was not a date." I gestured between us both. "Just two gym buddies having some food."

"Well, maybe one day, I will get you out on a date." He raised a brow. "In the meantime, let's get the check and I will see you around the gym, yeah? Unless of course you take me up on my offer of personal training or decide to change your times to avoid me again." He winked.

Looked like I was busted.

"You have my number, so if you ever want to go for a drink or to the movies, well…" He paused. "I'll leave it to you to decide."

I nodded. "Okay."

We left the restaurant and Garrett walked me to my car before bidding me goodnight.

It had boosted my mind and mood no end to have gone out with a good-looking guy for food and I drove home with a smile on my face.

CHAPTER THREE

Garrett

I'd been given the chance to move out of the standard student accommodation at King's and into the most premier accommodation on campus: Granger Lodge. The only problem was that to get a chance at the smallest room in the house—which was still four times larger than my present dorm room—I'd had to undertake and complete a series of challenges. Some of these challenges were not for the faint of heart and one in particular, involved a member of the opposite sex. However, I was a full-blooded male, and it was a one-off to score an amazing room. If the other roommates had asked me to sit in a bath full of their waste products for an hour, I would have done it. The other guys who lived there—seven, apart from myself—had all done the dares and pledged their allegiances to the house. It was a poor man's fraternity. Well, a few of us had a little money behind us, and my mate, Julian, probably had enough to buy the house itself.

It was Julian whose influence had got me an invitation to move in. I had known him from high school from where he had mysteriously disappeared before the end of term. However, a scandal involving a teacher and a pupil had paved the way for Julian's return to New York and he was studying computer science, before, he said, his father dragged him kicking and screaming into the political fold. From what I'd seen of Julian's behavior, I figured he'd make a fantastic politician. He believed half his own shit and played women like they were skittles and he was the bowling ball—they went down as soon as he touched them.

Anyhow, tonight at eleven was the final challenge, and I was to be escorted to the Dares Room for my final task, after which I would hopefully get my new room.

Even though I was usually an overconfident guy, this had me on edge. If I had to do something degrading to a member of the opposite sex, I was out of there. When I'd said this to Julian, he'd just laughed and told me to calm myself and stop sounding like a pussy. So, after college had ended, I'd taken myself off to the gym to get rid of the pent-up tension in my body. I'd looked for Meredith, but she hadn't been around. I'd breathed a sigh of relief. We'd only gone out for something to eat as friends, but it didn't sit well with me that I had been flirting with her and tonight I might have to do something with another woman.

I needed to avoid Meredith, anyway. I'd been shocked when she'd told me she was twenty-five and I'd quickly lied about my own age. The fact was I'd always looked way older than I was. The truth of it however was I'd recently celebrated my nineteenth birthday. If I'd told Meredith that, I would have never seen her again. I'd correctly guessed she would try to to avoid me after the incident where she'd almost fell off the treadmill, so lying about my age had been a no-brainer. I didn't know what the fuck I was doing, flirting with a woman who was way older than me. She was obviously nervous after being hurt in the past and she was a professor at my own college at that! Thank goodness I wasn't in any of her classes and our paths had yet to cross on campus. After we'd been out for our meal, I'd worn a ball cap low over my face when around campus, just in case.

I didn't know what I'd do if I met her again. I'd lied and told her I was a personal trainer and had given her my number. I totally doubted I'd ever hear from her, but the temptation to try had been too strong. If she called me, I could always tell her I was totally booked with clients. Oh, who the hell was I kidding? There was something about that woman. If she did contact me, I would carry on my charade, carry on lying. I just had to hope that her nervousness meant she didn't contact me, and she avoided coming to the gym at the same time as me from now on.

I pushed myself to my limits, showered, and headed back to my dorm room, where I dressed in some track pants and a tee, and then with my cap pulled low over my face again, I headed to Granger Lodge for my final challenge.

Julian let me in and then I was ushered into a room where it was explained that there would be a volunteer woman in the Dares Room and I would have to bring her to orgasm using my mouth and fingers. Her head would be covered in a mask and she could not speak, only moan. She'd be given a gesture that meant stop and one that meant she had come. I found it incredulous that any woman on campus would be willing to do such a thing, but Julian had organized it and what Julian Murphy wanted, Julian usually got. The Dares Room was fitted with a one-way mirror and the other guys would sit behind it making sure I did my challenge. I would be given a voice synthesizer to take in with me at first so I could tell the girl I was about to begin my dare and to use when she could leave.

I stood outside the room and took a deep breath. Was I really doing this? Then I recalled losing my virginity to Amy Johnson in 11th grade and figured it couldn't be worse than that. Let's just say I hadn't lasted long. Amy had had a cold and one of her sneezes had taken longer.

One of the older guys, Jacob, came out of the room. "All set," he said.

I placed my head in my hands and swallowed hard. "Could I get a glass of water? I'm not sure I can do this."

"Sure," Jacob answered. "Glass of water and then five minutes max for you to make your way into the room. There are plenty of other dudes willing to take your place."

When he handed me the glass of water, I closed my eyes and let it lubricate my mouth and throat. I had to fucking well hope that this girl wasn't someone who took forever to reach a climax, though Julian had said he didn't anticipate a problem. He'd told me the girl was from one of our classes, but that he would never tell me who she was and they would never know it was me. As far as the girl was concerned, she was meeting Julian in the room for some kinky play and knew it would be one of his mates she met, but not which one.

It was time. The guys got up from the couches to make their way to the room that had the viewing pane and Jacob opened the door to the Dares Room where a female laid atop the bed, a black gimp mask completely covering her face. She had on a black tee and a black pair of jeans. Using the voice synthesizer, I told her I was about to begin and that I was there for her own pleasure, not mine.

I took a deep breath. Fuck, this was really happening. I had to make this girl come and the guys would be watching. This was madness. But then again, the girl was willing and she got a come, while I got a new room. I mentally psyched myself up. Time to do this. I'd make sure she had a good time.

Reaching over, I unbuttoned the fastening at the top of the girl's jeans. I lowered the zipper, and she raised her hips for me as I lowered her jeans down her legs. The synthesized words, "What the fuck?" uttered from my mouth as I saw the unmistakable egg-timer tattoo that belonged to Meredith above her panties and recognized that athletic body now below mine. This was no girl from campus. How the hell was the professor in this room? What was Julian up to?

She sat up after I'd uttered my expletives, shaking slightly, and I stroked her shoulder.

"Sorry about that. I caught my finger in your zipper." I lied, so utterly thankful that she couldn't hear my proper voice. "Just lie back down and get ready for the time of your life."

Any reservations I'd had about the situation had now vanished. Beneath me, I was convinced I had the willing body of Meredith and I was not letting her go. I would deal with any repercussions that came after, but right now I was getting this girl to come in my willing mouth.

CHAPTER FOUR

Meredith

I skipped the gym that night and instead ate early, got myself changed into dark clothes and then hung around the apartment until it got later. Then I drove to campus. It was dark out by the time I arrived. I had my hair tied back into a bun, something I never wore at college, and I wore a pair of sunglasses that could easily pass for normal spectacles. There weren't many people around the vicinity of Granger Lodge, and I slipped unnoticed around the back of the property, to the room Marcus had shown on his map. Though my heart pumped hard, adrenaline boosted my intrigue of the situation rather than inhibit it. The thought I would bear witness to some horny goings on made my juices soak my panties. I got into position at the side of the window. It was seven minutes to eleven pm, and I had figured this was the time I needed to get in place. Neither too early nor too late. As Marcus had indicated, the blinds remained open, and the window was slightly ajar, with a space at the bottom.

A guy was talking to a girl in there. She had dark hair but was dressed similarly to me in a black tee and jeans. I must have turned fashionable overnight. I listened as he told her a guy would come into the room and give her an orgasm with his mouth and hands.

What?

He added that the girl's face would be covered so that she wouldn't see who it was, and I watched as the guy placed a black leather mask over her face, telling her the guy would be there in five minutes.

The minute he left the room, she ripped off the mask and sat there talking to herself. "You can do this, Stacey. It's for Julian. Come on, you can." No sooner were the words out of her mouth, I saw her dive toward the window. I quickly hid behind a tree as the window was raised further and Stacey climbed out and ran down the street.

I reckoned two minutes out of five had passed and very soon the mystery guy would walk into an empty room and be very disappointed. As was I. I quite liked the idea of being a voyeur and watching a couple get it on.

Then the thought came to me unbidden. She was dressed similarly to me and was wearing a mask. What if I went in the room instead of her? I had listened to the rules. She couldn't talk, and the guy had told her she would be given five minutes afterward in which to leave by the very window she had already escaped from. *No one would know it was me.*

Two minutes remained. I had no time to lose, and I quietly climbed through the window, placed the mask over my face, and kicking off my flats, I laid down on the bed.

The minute I laid there I decided this had to be the most impulsive, crazy thing I'd ever done. I would get caught, and I would be dismissed. I was going to let a student make me come. I'd finally lost my mind.

Then the devilish voice inside me had its turn to speak.

It's too late now, you're already here, and if you might get caught anyway. Why not enjoy yourself...?

I heard the creak of the door opening. This was it, the point of no return.

Footsteps walked closer to me.

"Please relax. I am about to bring you to orgasm.

I'm totally here for your pleasure, not my own." The voice that said the words was synthesized so that I couldn't know who it was. This pleased me. I needed the person who did this to remain faceless, nameless, voiceless. This was one of my students and it was so, so wrong. Yet the wetness pouring from my slick core, said it was oh, so right.

Fingers brushed the top of my waistband, my button was unfastened and then my zipper lowered. I raised my hips to help the person pull down my jeans, and then I heard their gasp and the words.

"What the fuck?"

I sat upright, wondering what was wrong. Did I have my name in my panties? Of course not. I wasn't at kindergarten.

"I'm sorry, I got my finger caught on your zipper," the voice said again, and I relaxed once more.

As fingers hooked the edge of my panties and lowered them down, I realized that the person in this room wasn't even necessarily male. I presumed they would be as the renters of Granger Lodge all were, something that harked back to arcane times and should have been kicked to the curb by now. But it could just as well be a female. All I was assured of was there would be fingers and a tongue; the rest was a mystery.

Panties off, my thighs were pushed apart by firm hands. I was pulled down to what I assumed was the edge of the bed and my ankles were placed over the person's shoulders. Every other one of my senses was amplified without the gift of sight. I could hear the low murmur of people outside walking around campus. In the room, there was the smell of old books—I'd noted a bookshelf with old looking novels on it when I'd got in —and the faint hint of aftershave, something that seemed familiar but that I couldn't place. It was probably what Marcus had worn.

"I will touch you now. I'm removing my voice changer and won't be talking again until the end. Please use your signals if you wish to end this and I'll stop straightaway," my mystery person stated.

I nodded my head and then a moan escaped my mouth as I felt first the gentle warmth from someone's breath and then a warm tongue licked its way up my soaking wet seam. I imagined it was a male doing this to me and at first, I pictured Marcus, but then I allowed myself to imagine it was Garrett from the gym. That my legs were wrapped around those firm shoulders and that it was that plump pink pout against my cunt and his tongue currently dancing around my pussy. His tongue licked over me in small circles, and it was so fucking amazing I thrust my hips up to meet it. Whoever was doing this, well, it wasn't their first rodeo. I'd had good sex in my time, but I'd never been tongue-fucked like this. The mouth left me, and my tee was pushed up. I quickly reached under and unhooked my bra at the back, freeing my pert, medium-sized breasts. I knew when I was aroused they went a dusky pink. A hand cupped around part of my breast and a fingertip flicked my nipple before fingers came together and pinched. I was almost delirious with the sensations coming over my body. The fact this was so damn naughty and wrong had made things ten times hotter than even the thought of being caught with Marcus in the staff room all those times previously.

A digit brushed my clit oh so slowly and I mewled. I wasn't sure a come from a mouth would be enough. I felt like I wanted to climb on top and ride a huge dick until I'd worn myself out.

The digit continued its torment for another minute or so and then dropped down into my heat and pushed into me. The finger was withdrawn and then a fuller sensation filled me, and I guessed I had two or three digits inside me now. They were slowly worked in and out, backward and forward and then a tongue to my clit was added to the equation. The tongue once again began its circular teasing and then my whole clit was sucked into his mouth. It was so very hard not to speak. I wanted to yell out the words, but instead I said them in my head.

Oh God, fuck me.

Drag me into whatever position you want in this room. I'm yours. Just make me come.

I want your hot tongue in my cunt.

Your dick, your massive dick riding me home.

My breathing was labored and was almost making me feel faint. I felt myself spiraling closer and closer to coming and as I did, the fingers left my pussy and his mouth fastened over my core. His tongue flickered quickly over my clit until it all became too much and I came, grasping his head and holding him firmly to my core before I flooded his face with my juices. Then I had to let his head go and move away as I was so sensitive that if he'd touched me there again, I'd have hit my head on the ceiling. I laid back capturing my breath, and I made the signal with my hand that said I was done.

A minute later the synthesized voice was back and they said, "Thank you. You are beautiful when you come." I heard footsteps, the sound lessening as they moved further away, followed by the opening and closing of the door.

Sitting up, I slid myself off the bed onto the floor and then I crawled in the direction of the window. I wanted no one to see my face if they came in, so I followed the direction of the breeze and the sound of the blind billowing until I felt the wall in front of me. Then I pulled off my mask and left back through the window. Once outside, I ran down past one of the other buildings until I found some steps where I sat and let myself readjust to the light.

My body trembled as I recalled my fingers trailing through shaggy hair as I held a mystery student's mouth against my pussy. *What the fuck had I done?*

CHAPTER FIVE

Garrett

I LEFT THE ROOM AND MET THE GUYS SPILLING OUT of the room with the viewing window. Now I would discover how the hell Julian had arranged for Meredith to be in the Dares Room.

"Nailed it," I said.

"What the fuck?" Julian replied, raking his hands through his hair.

I looked at him, my forehead furrowed in confusion. "I did what you asked, didn't I? She came like a firecracker."

"That wasn't Stacey," he stated. "I don't get it."

"Stacey?" I queried.

"Yeah, Stacey Sanders. The pussy I arranged to have in that room. Except it wasn't her."

"You saw who it was instead?" I asked, trying to keep the panic from my voice.

"I didn't see her face, but as she left through the window and pulled the mask off, her hair was blonde and in a bun. Stacey's a brunette."

"What the fuck are you talking about?" Jacob snapped. "I left Stacey in that room, just before Garrett went in. You're seeing things, having damn hallucinations. Told you to lay off the weed."

Julian shook his head. "If you hadn't all run out of here like pussies soon as she was done, you'd have seen the blonde hair for yourself and been able to back me up."

"Job was done. Now it's time to celebrate with our new roommate. Welcome to Granger House, Garrett." Jacob slapped me on the back.

The guys took it in turns to high-five me. When it came to Julian, I decided I needed to say something. I lowered my voice.

"I got the girls to switch. I wanted a pussy I knew. Hope it was okay and you'll keep it quiet, yeah?"

He shook his head. "You cheating bastard. I should throw you out on your ass. However." He high fived me. "Well played, man, well played."

We partied all night and I crashed in my new

room, even though all that was on my bed so far was a new mattress. It was a welcome present from Julian who said no one should ever have to endure some other dude's mattress. My thoughts had spun all night. How had Meredith got in that room? Where had Stacey gone? Did Stacey and Meredith know each other and had arranged a swap?

It didn't take too long to get some answers when I walked downstairs later the next morning, my mouth craving water and coffee like my life depended on it. Stacey was in the kitchen, her arms wrapped around Julian.

"Hey, Garrett. Congrats on your new room. Julian said he put in a good word for you. You're really lucky. This place is amazing."

"Thanks, Stace. Hey, do you know a professor called Meredith?" I asked. There was no time like the present.

Stacey's blank stare confirmed her answer before she did. "No, why?"

"She goes to my gym and apparently teaches here. I've not seen her, so I just wondered if you knew her seeing as you studied a different subject to us."

"No. Not one of mine. Not a fit person among them, believe me."

Julian's head tilted to one side and he gave me an appraising look.

"Someone got a crush? Hot was she? Thinking of changing from computer science when you find out what she teaches? Or is it something else you're wanting her to teach you?"

"Screw you. It would be me teaching her. I'm no saint in the bedroom."

"Did you hear that, Stacey? If Garrett got a crack at the professor, *he'd* teach *her*."

Stacey giggled. "Well, I've no idea who she is, but you're nineteen and she must be in her mid-twenties, so I reckon she'd eat you alive."

The thought of her eating me at all made my dick twitch.

"Well, I don't have a crush on her anyway. I was just intrigued if anyone knew her."

"Sure, we believe you," Julian whispered over the top of Stacey's head.

I spent the afternoon moving my belongings from my old dorm room into my fabulous new space. The bedroom also had closet space, a desk, bookshelves, an enormous flat-screen television, a wall-mounted sound system and gaming equipment. There was even my own refrigerator so I could keep beers cool in my room without them being drunk by the rest of the guys, and an en-suite bathroom.

I powered up my laptop and brought up the faculty. I clicked on the box marked 'staff' and typed

Meredith in the search bar. There was just one result and there she was, on screen, a smile on that pretty face, her long, blonde hair cascading past her shoulders. It stated Meredith Butler was professor of accounts and taxation.

Butler. Meredith *Butler*.

I sat back in my chair as I looked at her face on screen, the only part of her last night that I hadn't got to see. My hand rooted around below the waistband of my joggers until it fastened around my cock and while I stared at her photo, I imagined that I'd been able to fasten my mouth on hers last night. Then I recalled how I'd sucked her breast into my mouth and replayed her moans and groans in my head while she'd built up to that climax and how she'd exploded all over my mouth, her juices coating me. I'd licked my mouth clean, tasting her unique flavor.

In my fantasy, I imagined that she'd opened her legs for me and I'd sunk into her warm depths. As I pictured her warm flesh wrapped around my cock, I pumped my hand around my length. My cock had reacted violently to the thought of being sunk inside Meredith's pussy. It was rock hard. I picked up my pace, my breath quickening as I imagined her shouting my name as that explosive come pulsed around my cock instead of my mouth. I took my cock out of my joggers and fisted it hard until pressure built and I spurted streams of cum into my hand.

God, if this was what a thought did. How would the real thing feel?

How would our next meeting go? Would I tell her I knew it had been her in the lodge? Or was it entirely possible that I was mistaken, and it'd been another girl with the same tattoo? No. I shook my head. There might be more than one of those tattoos out there in the world, but not coupled with the exact same physique. It had definitely been her.

I couldn't start a relationship with a professor. She was six years older than I was, and if I maintained my appearance at the gym as a PT then I'd be basing anything that developed between us on a lie. Maybe it was better that I dated a girl my own age and forgot about my encounter with Meredith. Yeah, that was the way to go. Keep her as a memory in my spank bank.

My cell beeped and I picked it up to see who it was. There was no way I was going out again tonight, even if it was a Saturday night. I was still hungover and exhausted from the move.

Unknown number: Is that Garrett? I'd like to take you up on your offer of personal

training. Could you call or text me back? Meredith (from the gym).

Oh shit. Within ten seconds my resolutions had gone out of the window. I knew there was no way I was going to turn this woman down.

Garrett, the twenty-three-year-old PT it was. I was going to have to wear a ball cap on campus for the foreseeable future. I cleaned up and then sat back in front of the laptop. I had the rest of the day to cram personal training tips about running, so I could pass myself off as an expert the next day. Thank God, I'd excelled at track at high school.

CHAPTER SIX

Meredith

When I finally got my legs to stop trembling and resembling Jell-O, I made my way back to my car and stopped off at a drive-thru. My come down from all the adrenaline had made me ravenously hungry. Once home, I ate my food and then threw myself into the shower before changing into pajamas and getting under my comforter. I sat up in bed, resting against the headboard. I'd gone too far tonight. In the pursuit of seeking forbidden fun, I'd compromised my career. I needed a shrink.

I spent hours thinking through what I'd done. The problem was that I'd had an amazing experience, and the come of my life with a student, a faceless student. But what if the student had pulled off my mask?

I could never do anything like that again. Not in the college grounds. I'd taken risks with Marcus where I could have been discovered and now there was this latest reckless incident.

I realized I liked risky sex, a sense of the forbidden. It turned me the hell on. But I needed to find it outside of campus.

Garrett's face came to mind. He was twenty-three, to my twenty-five. It hardly made me a cougar, but it was a younger guy, right? Who knew what sort of sex he liked. As a personal trainer, he would have a serious amount of stamina. It was time I stopped avoiding potential relationships and got myself back out there. I needed a regular lover, one that could take me to the heights of passion. If they didn't fulfill me as a lover, like with Chad, then I would end it. No more Mr. Average for me. So, it was decided. I needed to date, and I would try to start with Garrett. I would ask him to train me and take it from there.

The next morning, I headed to the gym and worked out for a few hours, but Garrett never arrived. I hung around the cafeteria to grab a drink, disappointed that he wasn't there. I'd felt sure he would train on a Saturday morning. Then again, maybe he had private clients on weekends? I took my cell from my purse and sent him a message asking if he'd train me.

A few minutes later and I had a date and time: Central Park at 10am the next morning, to meet at the entrance across from the old FAO Schwarz building.

It was time to do some pampering to make sure I looked my best. I had a man to impress.

Fidgeting, I waited for Garrett to arrive. I was dressed in black shorts and a pink tee with a small, black fanny pack containing my car keys. It had a pocket holding a bottle of water, and I wore a band on my arm that my cell fitted in. I shuffled my feet from side to side, adrenaline battling against nerves because I didn't know how this day would go.

And then he was there. Jogging toward me. He was dressed in navy-blue shorts and a pale-blue tank. As he came nearer, I watched as the muscles in his thighs and calves rippled, displaying his immense strength and I soaked through my panties immediately. How pathetic was I? I gazed at the trees in the park and imagined him pressing me up against one, fucking me so my clothes shredded against the rough bark.

"Morning, Meredith."

"Call me, Mer," I told him. "That's what my friends call me. Well, when I had friends."

"Okay. Morning, Mer. Now what are you talking about? Lovely girl like you has to have friends."

"My best friend is now married and expecting a baby," I explained. "So, I'm kinda not doing too well on that front at the moment."

"Well, I'll be your friend, so now you have me." He smiled, a great big beam that lit up his whole face and made a shiver go up my spine as his gaze stayed on me. "Now, my friend, time to warm up."

He took me through warming up and then we went running around the park on a route Garrett had chosen for us. I thought I had a good current level of fitness, but it was clear from the get-go that Garrett could outpace me and leave me hanging way behind him if he so desired. He gave me some tips on picking up speed and I could see he really knew his stuff. By the time we had finished our session, I felt it'd been well worth it. My muscles and heart had experienced a serious workout.

"Shoot. How much do you charge? I hope I can afford you," I asked, realizing I should have started with this, rather than remembering at the end.

"You owe me nothing. As a friend your training is free," Garrett replied.

"No, I don't think so. I can't carry on with you training me unless you tell me what your hourly rate is and let me pay you." I stood with my hands on my hips so that he'd know I wasn't about to be overruled.

"Okay, well today is free." He held up a hand.

"Hear me out. Today is free because it's a trial. That's what I do for everyone who I train. One free session in order to see if we're a good fit. Do you think we're a good fit?" he asked, and I felt a blush rise to my cheeks.

"Seemed to be," I said to him, allowing myself to flirt a little.

"Great, well today you can pay me in coffee over there at The Grind." He nodded toward the coffee shop at the corner of the park. "Then we'll talk about future sessions and fees when we've got our breath back. Sound good?"

"Sounds great," I replied. "Race you to the coffee shop. Last one there is a loser." I took off before he realized what I'd said, but I knew he could still have beaten me if he'd wanted to. Yet he finished just behind me, grabbing me by the shoulder as we reached the coffee shop to try to drag me back and get past me.

"Damn, woman, only just," he said. His body was so near to mine, I swore I could feel the heat radiating between us. I stared up at him and he gazed down at me and something, *a look*, passed between us.

"What do you want to drink then?" he asked me, breaking the moment, and he headed past me into the coffee shop, leaving me salivating about his mighty fine ass that had just been in front of my eyes.

We took a seat inside. I would have preferred to sit near the window to get some fresh air, but Garrett insisted on sitting at the back, stating he wanted to be out of the sunshine. The darkness toward the back of the shop seemed more intimate. It made me nervous, and I rambled on, making conversation about nothing in particular.

"I want to ask you something, Mer." Garrett's gaze fixed on me.

"Er, okay."

"Would you let me take you on a date? A proper date, like to the movies or to dinner?"

I took a deep breath.

This was what you wanted, remember Meredith? Get back in the game.

I nodded. "Okay, yes. That would be nice."

"Nice? Ooh I can see I'll need to impress you more than I must be doing. I don't want our date to be nice, I want you so excited you can't sit still, not able to wait until we meet again."

My face must have frozen because he reached over to touch my hand.

"I'm joking. Shit, your ex really did a number on you, huh?"

I ran a hand through my bangs. "It's just been a while. I'll get there. Maybe I can sit on a bench full of ants so I can get that can't sit still feeling?"

We both laughed, and it helped break the tension.

"Now where would you like me to take you on our date?"

"Could we go to Olive Garden, maybe? Then to the top of Rockefeller? It's ages since I've done anything touristy. I've done Empire State, but I've never been up Rockefeller.

"Sounds like a plan. Well, actually, sounds like a date." He winked. "So, when is this date going to happen? Is tomorrow too soon?"

"Tomorrow sounds good actually, because I reckon I'll ache too much to go to the gym after today."

"Tomorrow it is then... and Mer?"

"Yeah?"

"Don't rule out the possibility of other things that could make you ache tomorrow."

I shook my head at him. "You are so bad."

He laughed. "I can't help it when I'm around you. My inner naughty boy comes out."

I feel my clit pulse—*naughty boy*—hell, yeah, I wanted one of those.

Calling his bluff, I brazened it out. "I would eat you alive, me being an older woman and all."

He raised an eyebrow at this and smirked, "I'm looking forward to tomorrow even more now."

We said our goodbyes, and I returned to my apartment where I loafed around on the couch, replaying the coffee shop conversation. I was really pleased with myself for flirting and not acting like a scared little mouse. I'd always had a rule that I never, ever put out on a first date, but after my tryst on campus, I decided to throw my stupid rules out of the window. If Garrett asked me back to his place tomorrow, I'd say yes; if not, I'd ask him if he wanted a coffee back at mine. My libido had decided to take center stage, and I was going to let it put on a show.

CHAPTER SEVEN

Meredith

On Monday, it was business as usual in the daytime and I went about my classes as normal, stopping for a break and meeting Tana for lunch on campus. We rarely got together these days, but I wanted to tell her my news.

She walked toward me. Her short, red medium-length bob blew in the breeze revealing a complexion that could color-coordinate with her hair. She looked green.

"Jeez, Tana, you okay?" I queried.

"I can barely move my head. Pregnancy sucks. If I move it too fast, I just want to hurl."

She sat on a bench next to me—slowly.

"Oh dear."

"Yup. I can look forward to at least another four weeks of this, possibly. Maybe even longer. It's worse than any drunken experience I've ever had. Everything smells, like way, way intense and strange. The fucking restrooms, dear God. Professor Trainor's irritable bowel has been playing up. I can't deal." She took in big breaths of fresh air. "This is lovely. Can't I teach outside?"

"I have a date," I interrupted her. We didn't get long for lunch and I didn't wish to sound mean, but she would spend all of it moaning about her pregnancy if I let her.

Tana twisted her head round to me quickly and groaned. "Bitch, if I'm sick on your shoes, it's your fault for giving me such a shock. You have a date? Who? When?"

"Tonight. His name's Garrett, and he's a personal trainer. I met him at the gym."

"Is he really, extremely, fantastically toned? Like mega hot bod, thick set arms, thighs that could crush bricks?"

"He so is."

"I'm insanely jealous. Wear your sexiest underwear and fuck his brains out. Ride him like an exercise bike."

"I was wondering what to wear."

"Oh, you got to do the whole polite thing first? Not just straight back to his for an *up close and personal*, personal training sesh? Boring." She bit on her lip. "Okay, well where are you going?"

"Olive Garden and then the Rockefeller Center."

"Skinny jeans and a tank, with a sweater to throw over your shoulders. A push up bra to make the most of those tits." She appraised me. "Ponytail, so if it gets breezy up top, you don't have hair in your face. Makeup but no lipstick. Your fringe will stick to it, plus hopefully you'll be locking lips with him. You don't want to look like Heath Ledger's Joker.

"You're the one with the green face."

"It's not fair, Don should have to take a turn. Men should have to do half the pregnancy."

"Yeah, I don't think that thought is worth having, babe."

She groaned again.

"Hey, at least you have the love of your life and a family on the way. My most intimate relationship is with my toothbrush."

Tana quirked a brow.

"With my mouth... for brushing my teeth... you dirty-minded woman."

"Well, you have time to change that now. Right, I'd better get back and see if I can make it through a class without running to the restroom. Don't drink too much tonight or you might be the same."

"I'm okay. There's a tutorial tomorrow morning with a guest speaker, so I don't have a class until eleven. Until then I will drink lots of coffee in the staff room under the pretense of marking textbooks."

"Lucky bitch."

We stood up, and I gave her a hug. "I hope it passes quickly for you, babe. Though you still look incredible."

"Really?" Tana answered perplexed.

"Well, like the Incredible Hulk, anyhow."

She punched me on the arm. "You made me move again. Speak soon." She dashed off, no doubt toward the nearest restroom.

I dressed as she suggested and I met up with Garrett outside Olive Garden. The meal passed quickly and easily. It was our first date but the third time we had drunk or eaten together and we had fallen into a relaxed pattern of ordering and conversation. We spoke about where we lived. Garrett shared with another guy so I took the hint that we wouldn't be going back to his apartment after our date.

"What about you?" he asked. "Where do you call home?"

"I have a small studio apartment in Brooklyn." I explained. "It's one big room with a separate bathroom. I really hope to get something bigger soon. I'm currently saving, but it will do for now. There is less room for me to mess up as I'm not the tidiest person."

"Seriously? I thought a teacher would be obsessional about having things in order," Garrett said.

"Workwise everything is on a desk in the apartment and I'm up to date. It's the rest of my life where it falls apart. For instance, my running kit from yesterday... well, there's a large chance I threw that at the bottom of my bed, and it hasn't made itself to the bathroom hamper yet."

"Are you telling me you're a dirty girl?" Garrett winked.

"Maybe." I winked back.

We split the bill at my insistence and walked toward the Rockefeller Center. After purchasing tickets, we went up in the fast elevator watching the neon show. It was still light and as we reached the top and walked out, I could see the vastness of Central Park and the rest of New York all around me. It made me realize how small me and my life were in the scheme of everything.

"What are you thinking?" Garrett had walked up

behind me and placed his hands around my waist pulling me closer to him. He'd spoken in my ear and it made me shiver. "Are you cold? Would you like my jacket?" he asked.

"I'm not cold, just sensitive to someone speaking that close to my ear," I replied. "Just thinking about how inconsequential we are. When you look at this vast space around us and think about all the people, the wildlife, the plants. We are such a tiny part of the planet and yet we think we're so important and that we have to be big achievers or somehow we have failed at life."

"Okay, so I will take these comments one at a time," Garrett said. "So, first, do you want me to stop speaking so close to your ear?" He ran his lips up the side of my neck and I rested my head back against him while my body erupted in goose bumps.

"No. Please carry on," I whispered.

"Good. Well, second, neither do I feel you are the slightest bit inconsequential." He tilted his hips slightly and there was no mistaking the hard erection brushing against my ass.

"And third, yes, we are all a tiny part of the planet. But I don't believe we've failed should we not make major accomplishments in life. If you end up settled and happy with your lot, then I think you're a winner." He paused. "However, I do believe that we take life for granted and so we shouldn't wait if we see something we want. Why waste days or opportunities? Sometimes you have to take life by the horns and ride that devil."

I pushed back against his erection. "Are you sure you're not mixing up horns with horny, and are you the devil you're suggesting I ride?"

"I've wanted to fuck you since the day I met you at the gym," he whispered in my ear.

I turned around, so that his rock-hard cock rested against my center as I put my hands around his waist. "This view is amazing, but would you like to see the view of the inside of my apartment now?"

"Hell, yes. The view inside your apartment and the view between your legs. I'm sure that'd be much more entertaining than the view from up here."

"You're not enjoying it up here?" I asked him.

"The view is amazing," he said looking at me. "Both out there and right here." Then he dipped his head closer to mine and brushed his lips across my own in a quick sweep. When they traveled back to mine a second time, he deepened the kiss, crushing his mouth against my own. My mouth opened slightly, and his tongue dipped in tasting me.

I felt the swell of my breasts and the hardening of my nipples beneath my tank and broke off to cover myself with my sweater.

Garrett grabbed hold of my hand and led me back toward the elevators. It was time to go home.

We shared a cab back to mine. I hadn't driven in case I'd wanted to get wasted. If this date had gone bad, I felt sure I'd have looked for the answers to life via the bottom of a wine bottle.

But it hadn't gone bad and I was looking forward to seeing what the rest of the evening brought. Hopefully, many, many orgasms.

CHAPTER EIGHT

Garrett

If I'd had the opportunity, I would have slapped myself around the face to see if I was dreaming. I was on my way to Meredith Butler's apartment. My horniness far overrode my need to be honest with her about my age. The only actual lies I'd told her were about my age and about my career as a personal trainer. I lived in a room share in Manhattan, that wasn't an untruth. I just omitted it being on the college campus. She was exuberant about her job and about accounting and I'd wished I could join in with discussions about business, but she thought I was a PT and so I kept the subject around fitness.

Meredith's apartment was small, but it wasn't the

dump I'd expected. Yeah, sure, she picked up a few things when we first walked in, but not much. Christ, if she saw my place on a Saturday morning she would die.

"I'm just going to freshen up in the bathroom. There's a bottle of wine and some beers in the refrigerator if you'd like to get them."

I nodded and headed toward the tiny kitchenette where I extracted two cold beers. After rummaging in a couple drawers, I located a bottle opener, opened the bottles, and then I placed both drinks on a small coffee table in front of the couch.

When Meredith came out of the bathroom, I swallowed deeply. She was wearing just a lacy black bra with a small pink bow in the center and a matching thong. That taut body with her trademark tattoo was exposed to me again for the second time in four days—not that she knew that. I needed to ensure that I didn't repeat any moves from Friday night. I didn't want her knowing it was me, not yet. If our relationship went the distance—if we somehow made it past a few dates—then I'd confess all, but right now I wanted her to know what she'd miss if she let me go because of my age. Truth was, I wanted her hooked on me. I lifted my bottle and took a pull on my cool beer to wet my throat which had gone so dry.

"You look beautiful," I told her truthfully. "Now

come sit here with your beer while I go freshen up myself."

I passed her as I headed into her bathroom and it took all of my self-control to not grab her and push her up against the wall. In the bathroom, I stood in front of the mirror where I looked at myself, trying to see what she saw. No way in hell did I look nineteen years old. No way in hell was I going to act it either.

I went out of the bathroom and Meredith looked up, unsure as to what would happen next.

"Stand up," I commanded.

She did, and I hoisted her up and placed her over my shoulder where I spanked her bare ass cheeks.

"It's playtime," I told her. "Time to show you you're mine."

I placed her on the bed and instructed her to stay on all fours with her ass raised high in the air. Then I peeled off her bra and panties so that she was completely exposed to me while I stayed fully dressed. Kneeling behind her on the bed, I enjoyed the view of those creamy tits hanging down, and that firm white ass in the air, her puckered hole on display. I'd claim that another time. Right now, I fastened my mouth on her pussy and played her like a piano. I knew the moves that made her come and from this different position she couldn't place her hands in my hair. I didn't do the circular motion from before; instead, I trailed my tongue in the letters of the alphabet, one after another until O really was for orgasm and she came against my mouth in a shudder.

Quickly, I stripped off my own clothes and guided her off the bed, toward her wall, not giving her a moment to recover. I feasted on her lips, letting her taste herself on my tongue and then I pushed her legs apart and slammed my cock in her still pulsating cunt.

"Oh my fucking god," she screamed out.

With every thrust she hit the wall behind her. I hoped her neighbors heard. I hoped the world heard and knew she was mine. The thought made me bite her neck—mine—I wanted to mark her.

"Garrett," she squealed. "I have to work tomorrow, don't leave me with visible marks."

I lowered my head and sucked part of her breast into my mouth biting and marking that instead. In response, she scratched her hands up my back so hard it should have made me cuss, but it was all a mingle of pleasure and pain and I couldn't get enough.

"Now what will they think to those scratches in the gym?" I whispered in her ear.

Her hooded gaze captured my own. "They'll think you have a passionate lover and they'd be right."

I turned her around and pressed her up against the wall, her breasts hitting the coldness of it, making her gasp. Strumming her clit with my fingers, I simultaneously restarted my thrusts. I could feel the strength in her body as we pushed against each other chasing our climaxes.

"Do you want me, Mer?"

"Yes."

"How? Tell me what you want."

"I want you to fuck me, hard."

Then she said something I really was not expecting.

"I want you to move us to the window and fuck me against it so someone might see."

I stilled for a moment and felt her tense.

"It's okay," she said quietly. "I got carried away."

I turned her back around to me and with my fingers on her chin I tilted her gaze to make her look at me.

"Do you want me to fuck you against the window? I will do anything you want, Mer. Anything."

"Yes," she answered meekly.

"Look at me and don't be embarrassed about asking for what you want. What do you want me to do? Say it again," I commanded.

"Garrett, I want you to fuck me against the window."

I picked her up again and moved toward her window. It looked out over some other apartments and there was a pretty good chance someone would see what we were doing. Neither of us cared. I pressed her against the glass of the window which was actually a door that led out onto a balcony. It was just enough that visibility would be hazy. I pushed her against it, her tits splayed out against the glass. I had her arms raised and held above her head by my left hand. My right hand went back between her thighs bringing her closer and closer to the edge.

"Is this what you wanted, Mer? People could be watching you. Do you like the thought of that? The risk. Do you like knowing you might be caught?" I thought about how she'd taken Stacey's place in the lodge and now I got a hint as to what had placed her there that day. She must have seen Stacey leave and decided to take her place. I still had questions about that evening though. How had she known what Stacey was there for? Then Meredith groaned and my mind came back to the present time.

I nibbled at her neck with my lips, careful not to leave a mark. She shivered under my touch.

"I need you. I need you so much. Please, please fuck me harder, Garrett."

How could I resist that? I quickened my pace and as she pressed into the window, it made a squeaking sound as her body rubbed against it. Wetness flooded from her pussy around my cock. She was that turned on. I let go of her hands and I grabbed a fistful of her hair and pulled as I emptied myself into her, spurts of cum erupting from me. Meredith let herself go. She screamed my name as she came, those strong pulses milking my cock. It was everything I had fantasized about and more. I just needed to convince her this was not wrong. That we were man and woman, not student and teacher. But for now, I wasn't done with Meredith Butler. I carried her to the bed where I fucked her another twice. I'd never tire of hearing her scream my name.

We had fallen asleep, her snuggled in the crook of my arm. She stirred which woke me and I looked at the digital clock on her nightstand which told me it was six am. Fuck, I needed to get home and get ready for college.

I moved my hand slowly from underneath her and she stirred again, her eyes fluttering open. I watched as her eyes focused on mine, seeing the realization as to where she was and who she was with hit her memory bank. Then a smile crept across her face.

"What time is it?" she mumbled.

"Six, and I need to get ready."

She pulled herself upright. "Me too. I forgot to set the alarm. I usually get up at this time anyhow."

"Do you have a shower every morning?" I asked her.

"Yeah." She nodded. "Why?"

"Because I reckon we can get showered together and save time."

"I doubt it will save time, Garrett," she replied and laughed.

I eventually got back to my place around seven am. Some of the guys including Jacob were in the kitchen.

"Dude, you get a place here then stay out all night? Must be some sweet pussy you tapped."

I winked at him. "I'd better get to my room and get my books together fast, or I'll be late to class. Pour us a cup of Joe, will you? I'm dead on my feet. It was a hard night if you catch my drift."

Jacob high-fived me, "Dude, I'm so jealous. Cassie won't talk to me right now. My balls are gonna burst if she doesn't relent soon."

I took my coffee up to my room. I had a clear thirty minutes where I could kick back. Playing some music low, I sat back on the bed. So, Meredith liked a little kink. I could work with that. The only thing I would struggle with, however, was paying for all of our dates. I was getting an allowance from my father while I did my course after which there would be a job for me. I'd offered to take a paid job alongside studying, but my father wouldn't hear of it, telling me it was only fourteen months. He'd said he and my mom had spent their money on me for nineteen years, what was a little longer.

He'd already be at work now and I decided to give him a call. I was very close to my dad.

"Hey, Dad."

"Garrett. To what do I owe this pleasure so early in the morning? You in trouble, son?"

"No, Dad. Just had some time to kill before college, so what better way to spend it than to talk to my old man. Mom all right?"

"Your mom's fine. Driving me crazy as usual. Now she won't let me eat mac and cheese. She needs to stop watching these stupid diet shows."

"So, let me guess. You're pretending to go along with it."

"Course, son. Then I call at Marge's cafe and eat it there, every damn lunchtime. That's what you do with women, you let them think they're winning. Saves you a headache."

My parents had been married almost thirty years. I was the youngest child at nineteen. I had an older sister aged twenty-five and a brother at twenty-nine. My siblings both worked alongside Dad. It was a proper family business, except for my mom, who said the only bottleneck she was interested in held wine. Computers weren't her thing.

"I'm just looking at your account online, son. You spent a little more than usual last couple days."

Really, I should have known he'd check up on me because of my call.

"I met someone, Dad. I've shouted her a few coffees and dinner, but we went out last night and she insisted we split the bill."

"Sounds like a keeper."

"Well, I've only known her a week, so it's a little early to say, but I really do like her."

"What's she do?"

"She's an accountant." I skipped over her being a professor of accounts at my college. I wasn't ready to go there yet. "She's a few years older than me."

My dad whistled. "You got yourself one of those cougars, do you?"

I laughed, "She's not that old."

"Well, listen," he said. "I just added a couple hundred bucks to your account, because I think if you found a nice lady, you need to take her out and treat her right."

"Thanks, Dad."

"No need to thank me, son. I'll deduct it from your wages when you start here."

He burst into hearty guffaws. It was so good to hear his voice.

"Well, I'd better go get ready for class. Now, why

don't you make that mac and cheese just twice a week and I'll not tell Mom?"

"You're a devil, Garrett James. I do you a good turn and you come back at me with a forked tongue. Now, treat that lady with respect and if it carries on, well, me and your mom would love to meet her sometime."

"Okay, Dad. Speak soon. I love you."

"Love you too, son. Now get to class."

I ended the call with a smile on my face. My family thought nothing of stating our feelings for each other and I loved that. I thought about Mer saying she was short of girlfriends and wondered about introducing her to my sister sometime. They were the same age. Then I sighed. I wouldn't be able to introduce them until I'd told Mer my real age and after that she might not want to see me again. Sighing again, I got up off the bed and drank down my coffee. I changed into some fresh clothes and grabbed my backpack, slipping my feet inside some chucks. Once downstairs, I paused in the kitchen to pinch a bagel out of Jacob's hand and then I was on my way to class. I remembered my ball cap as I was leaving, took it from my backpack and pulled it down low once more.

"Is this a Justin Bieber look, or some shit like that?" asked Julian, who had caught me up just outside the door to walk across campus. "You trying to be all cool?

Or are you avoiding someone? Either way, you look a dick."

"It's the Bieber thing, I'm a Belieber." I rolled my eyes at him.

"Well at least if Prof. Geller pukes in the wastebasket again you can pull that over your face away from the sight. God, the smell," he said.

"Yeah. Also her being pregnant means we'll get a tutor change partway through the course too. I hope her replacement will be as good as she is. I need to pass this course so I can start earning. Student life is not for me."

"At least you get to decide what you want to do. I'm just instructed by my parents, like I'm a robot."

"That sucks. You'll have to get that sorted, Julian. Your life is yours, not theirs."

"Yeah, well, I'll get this course passed and see what's next. I have to know about computers you know. One day I might be in charge of The White House." He snorted.

We reached the classroom.

"Well, for now, President Murphy, get yourself sat down while you wait for the call from the current president to say he's ready for you to step up."

I sat at my desk and unpacked my gear ready for the start of the lesson.

"Looks like we have a replacement already." Julian

commented. "Fuck, she can teach me any time. I've never seen her around here before."

I looked up and froze in horror. How could this be? She didn't teach this subject. She had no need to travel across this side of campus. Why was she at the front of the class now flicking through papers?

"Good morning, everyone." That familiar voice spoke. "My name is Professor Butler. Professor Geller has been taken ill and won't be with you this first lesson. However, she has passed me the lesson plans and we can do a revision session, so if you'd like to get your computers fired up."

It was at that point Julian decided he'd had it with my 'under the radar' persona and he knocked my ball cap straight off my head. "I can't deal with talking to the peak of your cap, man. I wanna see your face."

"Could you keep it down over there," Meredith yelled and then I saw her eyes flit from Julian's and settle on mine. All the blood drained from her face.

"Excuse me a moment," she said and then she ran out of the room.

"Fuck, is this one pregnant too?" quipped Julian.

CHAPTER NINE

Meredith

I ran straight into the bathroom where I threw up that morning's breakfast. My body shook as the mental image of Garrett, there in the classroom, came back to my mind.

He was a student.

In a class of eighteen and nineteen-year-olds.

Fuck, this couldn't be happening.

When I was convinced there was nothing left for me to vomit, I walked with trembling legs over to the basin where I splashed my face with cool water. My cell phone vibrated in my pocket and I took it out. I knew who the message would be from.

Garrett: I've left the class. Made an excuse. Go back and teach. No need for you to get in any trouble.

Trouble? God, I was already in trouble. I had slept with a student which was against the college's strict policies. I spent a few more minutes composing myself, reapplied some makeup and then I returned to teach the class, giving the excuse that I'd skipped breakfast and had felt lightheaded.

At lunch, my cell vibrated again.

Garrett: I need to see you. To explain.

I typed a message back.

Mer: What's left to explain? You lied. You're not a personal trainer at a gym. I'm a fool.

He replied within a minute.

. . .

Garrett: You wouldn't have dated me if you knew my real age. You can't say we aren't perfect together. That would be the LIE.

I placed my cell back in my pocket. Right now, I couldn't deal with him and what had happened. I needed to think. He was right; we seemed good together. But I was several years older than him and it wasn't allowed.

Oh my god. Why was the thought it wasn't allowed exciting me, rather than worrying me?

I needed to get to class to teach. That's where my focus should be. I threw the rest of my lunch in the trashcan and went to my next lesson.

As I left that night a thought came to mind and so I sent another text to Garrett.

Mer: Please don't turn up at my apartment tonight. I need time to think.

The reply was swift.

. . .

Garrett: I'm already outside waiting for you.

Goddamn it!

Mer: Please leave. I need time.

Garrett: I can't do that. We need to talk.

Mer: I have nothing to say to you right now.

Garrett: Then just listen.

Mer: I need to get my head straight. I'm a mess. I keep making mistakes that could cost me my job. Please tell me you'll leave.

There were no messages for a few minutes, and I sat in the driver's seat of my car waiting. I wasn't going home until he'd agreed to leave. Then the final message came, which gave me my second huge shock of the day.

. . .

Garrett: I would know that body anywhere, even when your head is obscured by a mask. I drank in your juices like the sweetest honey. Don't you want more?

He was the guy from the Lodge?

I thought back to the student who had made me come. How I had run my hands through his hair. Yes, it could have been Garrett. How would he have known I was there anyway if he hadn't been in the room? It was stupid, but I was relieved. At least there was only one student I'd conducted an inappropriate relationship with now. I decided that I might as well travel back to my apartment. I doubted that Garrett would leave without talking to me and I needed to know what had happened that night. Why he was in a room ready to mouth fuck a student. My chest felt tight at the thought of him doing what he had done to me to another student, and at that point I knew I was screwed.

I really liked him.

And as a lover he was unbeatable.

I walked to my apartment door and Garrett rose from his seated position on the floor. He shook out his legs that were no doubt cramped from his previous position.

The ball cap wasn't anywhere in sight, and he ran a hand through his hair, his expression tortured.

I put a finger to my lips. "Wait until we get inside."

I unlocked the apartment door and walked inside, throwing my purse and laptop bag onto the desk and walking over to the window to let in some air. Then I got two bottles of water from the refrigerator and handed one to Garrett, nodding toward the couch.

"Okay," I told him. "I think what I need right now is brutal honesty. From yourself and from me. Talk to me from the start of us meeting. Did you know I was a professor at your college?"

Garrett shook his head. "No. When you slipped from the treadmill, I'd never seen you before, but... I know this sounds dumb... but I felt a connection to you. It wasn't until we went to the restaurant after the gym that you told me what you did and where. By then, it was too late. I'd already fallen for you."

"So, what were you doing in Granger Lodge?"

"I live there."

"What?" My fingers touched my parted lips.

"I live there. I moved in Saturday morning, so I've lived there two whole days."

"What was Friday night about?" I knew of course

from Marcus, but I wanted to hear whether Garrett would tell me the truth.

"That was my final challenge to win my accommodation, but then you must have known that to be in the room..."

He left his sentence hanging.

"I need wine," I told him. "Water will not cut it."

Returning with a bottle of red and two glasses, I poured my own and left the other glass and bottle there. Garrett could get his own.

I sat back on my side of the couch and curled my legs under myself.

"I used to, God, how do I define it? After college sometimes I used to stay behind with one of the male professors. He left at the end of the last year. We'd make out in the staff room, give each other satisfaction."

"Did you fuck him?" Garrett's jaw tightened, and a tic pulsed in his cheek.

"Once. A goodbye fuck when he was leaving." I stared across the room for a moment as Garrett's gaze was too intense. I felt like he was burning me. "He left me a letter. Told me that Granger Lodge had a kinda initiation that was sexy..." My voice trailed off and I took a slug of wine before continuing. "He knew I liked the risk, the thought of being caught. That was what had turned me on in the staff room, more than him. He was just a body. It was the idea of getting caught that made me come."

"So how did you end up in the room?" he asked.

"I watched the girl panic. She climbed through the window and ran away. It was a split-second impulsive decision to take her place. Crazy. I could have been caught and lost my job."

"But the thought of the experience won?"

"Yes. The thought that someone unknown was coming into that room and would make me come and they wouldn't have a clue who I was."

He smiled. "Except it was me and I recognized your tattoo."

I clutched my blouse where my tattoo lay underneath. "I never gave that a thought. That's how much I had thought it through. An easily identifiable tattoo and I just lay there."

"You didn't just lay there," he said. "You moved against me like we were a violin and bow."

I moved my legs, making out they were going dead when in fact his words had made me itch to rub my thighs together.

"Then you knew I was a professor at the same business college as you, but you said nothing anyway?"

He shook his head. "When I got a text the next morning asking if I'd meet you to train you, I had to go.

I had to see the woman again who'd exploded against my mouth.

A pathetic half-laugh escaped my mouth. "And I texted you because I thought I should try to engage in a relationship with someone around my own age."

"Age is just a number," Garrett snapped. "I'm still the same guy you fucked last night. A man, not some little boy, so don't even think of treating me like one."

I sighed. "I know exactly what you are, Garrett, that's the problem."

"And what's that?" he said, looking hurt, like I was about to destroy him with my words.

"You're my downfall," I said and then I drank the rest of the glass of wine.

This time Garrett told me his real history. How his father ran a computer science company that looked into how systems could be run smoother and more efficiently. In just over fourteen months, Garrett would take a job at the family firm alongside his elder brother and sister. Fourteen months. That was how long we would have to stay a secret if I continued this.

"Is there anything else you want to know about me, Meredith?" Garrett finished his water. He'd not touched the wine. I felt the buzz of the alcohol in my system, making me feel mellower. Making me give less of a fuck about anything.

"If you'd been told to fuck the girl in the room to

get your new accommodation... would you have done it?"

He stroked his chin. "Before I met you, yes, without a doubt. I'm young. As long as she had consented, and we had a good time, why not?"

I looked at the floor.

"But after, I don't know. I was prepared to go down on the girl and give her a good time, but to fuck someone, when all I had in my mind was you. I'd have been using them. Because I'd have imagined your face under that mask whether it was you or not."

"I imagined it was you," I confessed. "Yours was the face I held in my mind while the stranger got me off." I shook my head. "And it was you all along. I want to replay it," I told him. "Now that I know it was you. I want to do it again."

He pulled me toward him, brought my face closer to his. "Yes, but this time, I will do what I wanted to do after you came on my face. I want to fuck you until you're no use to anyone else because you'll crave only me.

Straddling him on the couch, my breasts pressed against him through my blouse. I ground my pubic bone against his groin while my mouth captured his. Garrett fisted his hands in my hair and then showed his strength again when stood up with me still wrapped around him like a monkey on a tree. He walked a few paces and then he threw me down onto my bed. I watched as he looked around the room until he spotted a scarf I'd left at the foot of the bed, another item that had yet to make it to the laundry hamper. He picked it up and fastened it over my eyes. I was returned to Friday night and not being able to see, everything being left to my other senses, my being alert, but this time I didn't have to imagine it was Garrett, because it *was* Garrett, had been him all along.

He stripped me out of all my clothes. I felt the cool breeze from the window flick over my body, making my nipples peak and my skin goose bump. Large hands gripped my breasts and tweaked my nipples and then I felt his tongue *there*, it was so definitely him. I placed my hands in his hair, the hair I now recognized while he traced his tongue in the lazy circles that had made me come so hard before.

Fingers entered me, plunging into my heat while his tongue continued to tease and torment me. I was already riding so close to the edge, and it had only been a few minutes. As I exploded over his mouth, he repeated the words I'd heard Friday night.

"You are beautiful when you come."

And then I came again, a second wave following the first as I bucked against Garrett's mouth giving him everything I had. I remembered all the thoughts and feelings I'd had on the Friday night, how I'd wanted to ride a huge cock. How the tongue hadn't been enough.

"Please, I need to feel you inside me," I begged.

"I need to be inside you. My dick is so fucking hard. Feel what you do to me."

He moved up the bed and placed his dick in my hand. I felt the girth of him. He was wide, and he was long. I twisted so that he got the message I wanted to ride him and then I climbed on top of him. I positioned his dick at the entrance to my soaking wet pussy and then I lowered myself onto that huge cock.

As he lifted his hips and impaled me deeper, I moaned and groaned. I was full of cock and I loved it. He brought his fingers to my clit and teased me there while I put one hand on his toned stomach and another in my hair and I raised myself up and down on his huge pole, changing to flicking my hips in tiny circles, feeling him plunging deeper and deeper inside my walls. I moved a hand from my hair to one of my breasts and cupped myself there, rolling my breast in my hand before teasing my nipple and then swapping to the other side.

"Garrett, I'm so close."

Just when I thought I had everything I wanted, Garrett spoke.

"Look at you, you dirty bitch. Open your eyes. You're fucking me. Fucking a student. We're in the classroom. Can you see that? We're in the classroom and I'm fucking you on your desk and the other students could come in at any moment. And you don't care. You're just riding my cock and ready to explode and I can hear footsteps coming up the hall and we're about to be caught at any time."

My clit and walls started to pulse slowly around his cock as I felt my climax explode around him. I went off like a firecracker.

"Oh my fucking god."

Garrett held onto my ass firmly with those huge hands that belonged to those super strong arms and he rode me through my orgasm until he spilled with his own, cum shooting inside me. I collapsed forward onto his torso, sweat pouring down my face. My breathing was ragged and my heart pounded so hard I feared a cardiac arrest.

"That was what I wanted to do to you Friday night." Garrett said, stroking my hair back and holding it off my face. "Don't tell me this is wrong, because it doesn't feel wrong. It feels all so right."

I looked up at him and bit my lip. I craved him, but I knew I shouldn't continue this.

"And next time, we really will fuck in a classroom," Garrett added.

And I was done for.

CHAPTER TEN

Meredith

Of course, I was the one with the classroom...

I told him where I'd be and agreed to text him when there was no one around.

That day I'd deliberately dressed as a stereotypical college teacher in a white blouse and tight skirt, but before I texted Garrett, I added some clear lens spectacles and put my hair up in a bun.

Mer: It's time for your lesson.

. . .

A text came straight back.

Garrett: Yeah, we'll see who teaches who!

I knew it wouldn't take long for him to arrive, now I knew he lived on campus. While I waited, I sat back in my seat, my mouth going dry. After a few minutes the door opened quietly, and he stepped inside. All the blinds on the windows were closed. I had switched on a small desk lamp which gave a low glow and a look of warmth to the room.

"I've come for my detention," said Garrett.

"You've been a very bad boy," I told him walking around the front of my desk. "You do not stroke your cock in my classroom, do you understand that?"

"Yes, Professor," he replied.

"Now I want to know what was causing you to be so distracted in my class."

"You, Prof."

"Say that again. I'm not sure I understand. Explain yourself."

"You, Prof. I watched you at the front of the classroom and when you wrote on the top of the blackboard, I could see the tops of your stockings."

I lifted my skirt to reveal the lacy tops of my stockings. "These?"

Garrett put his hands across his pants to cover his dick. "Yes, Prof."

"Why are you covering yourself, Garrett?"

"I have an erection."

"Show me."

Garrett unbuckled his belt and unfastened the zipper of his pants. As he lowered them his dick sprung against the material of his boxers. He was so hard. I walked over to him and dropped to my knees.

"Would you like to feel my mouth around your cock, Garrett?"

"Yes, Prof."

It would be the first time I had given oral to Garrett, and I couldn't wait. My panties were soaked with my cum. I lowered his boxers down his legs, and he lifted each foot in turn so I could remove them.

"Garrett, have you been hiding this big dick from me all year?"

"Yes."

I took him in my hand and lifted him to my mouth. His cock was a deep purple and so hard. I opened my mouth and took him deep inside, closing my lips around him and sucking. He grabbed the back of my neck.

"Fuck, Meredith."

I slid him in and out of my mouth, licking around his glans, one hand cupping his balls. I ran my fingertips lightly across them. As he got closer to climax and started thrusting more firmly into my mouth, I moved a hand behind his ass, cupping a firm cheek. I could feel his ass cheek undulate under my fingers with each thrust. My face was aching from all the sucking, but I wasn't letting him go until he'd given me his all.

"Mer. Christ, Mer, I'm gonna—"

I stuck my finger in his ass and he spurted his salty cum straight down my throat. I swallowed it down and looked up at him. His eyes were closed while he savored what had just happened.

"Shit, Mer. That was incredible."

"For using my first name and not calling me Prof, you will have to be punished," I told him, winking.

"What's my punishment? I'm already in detention." he asked.

"Because of your attitude you will fuck me in the ass, Garrett."

"I'm gonna be bad much more often," mumbled Garrett, and I tried hard not to laugh, but eventually a small snort escaped my mouth.

Garrett led me back toward my desk, pulled up my skirt and turned me over.

"First, I need to make you wetter," he said.

I wasn't sure that was possible, but then I realized he meant to lube around my puckered hole. He tore off my panties like they were made of thin paper and then used a hand to tease some of the wetness from my pussy up to my ass and he slid inside my pussy coating himself in my juices. I pushed back against him.

"I don't remember saying you could put that there."

He bit the back of my shoulder in response.

His fingers, coated in my cum, played around my butt hole and then he inserted a finger inside me. I groaned.

"Oh, you like that do you? What about two?" he asked. He did what he promised and two and then three fingers were in my butt thrusting and twisting inside.

His fingers withdrawn, Garrett withdrew his cock from my pussy and positioned himself next to my ass and pushed in. At first there was resistance, but as he teased me there and as the fingers from his other hand dipped into my pussy, I relaxed and he edged in further, inch by glorious inch.

I moved back against him and took in the rest of his cock in my ass.

He fucked me oh so slowly while his fingers trailed up inside my blouse until they found my breasts. He pulled down the front of my bra and flicked fingertips across my hardened nub. Then he moved me slightly so that my pussy was against the rounded corner of the desk. As he thrust in my ass, he pushed my clit into the edge of the table. It gave me a tease of friction in my clit, but I wanted more. He repeated his motions over and over again.

"You're fucking my cock and the desk, you dirty professor."

"I need to come so bad," I almost shrieked.

He thrust harder in my ass so that again my clit met the edge of the desk and as he quickened his motions, my pussy rode the desk edge. Tomorrow I would be in this class teaching, sat at the very desk I was pounding with my pussy while my lover pounded my ass. I felt the telltale quivers starting in my core and then I came. Garrett stuck his fingers in my pussy as I did, so that my walls clamped around him as I shuddered my release.

"Oh my god."

Garrett leaned his head on my back. "That was fucking amazing, Prof."

I laughed. "That's one fantasy met. Now I have another."

"You're so greedy." He kissed the back of my neck. "What's your next one?"

"That I ride my lover's dick all night long. Come to

mine Friday so I can make it come true. We can stay in bed and sleep Saturday."

But what happened was we saw each other every night. We never saw the inside of a gym; we spent all our time burning calories on each other. We were insatiable. I couldn't get enough of him. I'd get home from class, and he'd be there. My marking wasn't getting done, all thoughts of work forgotten. In the classroom, I could barely keep my eyes open. After a couple of weeks, I was asked to meet with the principal one afternoon.

I walked into his office and took the seat he indicated.

"Meredith. I just wanted to check in with you. There have been a few complaints from students about the level of teaching they are receiving. Also, they are concerned about you. You're coming to class bleary-eyed, tired. Work isn't being assessed. Is there anything I should know about?"

All I could do was lie. "I've been trying to hide the fact I've had a virus. It's nothing major, but it's wiped me out a little. I apologize for the fact you've had to deal with complaints about me."

"It's been more concern that complaints. Your

students care about you and know what a high standard you usually expect from them alongside your own commitment. Look, I appreciate you trying to carry on while ill, but I think it would be better if you took a few days off. Come back after the weekend when hopefully you'll be back to your usual self."

I nodded. "Thank you, Professor Lynch. I think I'll do that."

"I have the rest of the week's classes covered. Go home and get some rest."

"Thank you again. It's appreciated."

He smiled. "Look after yourself, Meredith."

I went home, but I didn't get any rest. Instead, Garrett called in sick to college.

On Sunday, I went against what my heart and body craved, and I sent Garrett home. It took until one pm that afternoon to get him out of my apartment, but eventually he left, knowing that he also needed to get his act together. His own grades would fall if we carried on this way and his future job with his father depended on it. His family were paying a lot of money to put him through this course. I couldn't have his failure on my conscience. I couldn't have my own students failing or falling behind because of me either. My behavior was inexcusable. I was like a young girl with a stupid crush. I spent a few hours in bed catching up on some much-needed sleep, then I showered and set to work on catching up on some marking. From now on, even though it would be difficult, we needed some space away from each other. I vowed that I'd only see him every other night. He was becoming an addiction, my drug of choice, and if I wasn't careful, he would destroy me or I him.

CHAPTER ELEVEN

Garrett

"What was the fucking point giving you a room at Granger Lodge when you're never fucking in it? Who are you boning and what's with all the sneaking around and skipping college?"

I might have known Julian would be savvy enough to know I wasn't around and was acting out of character.

"I'm going to be around more now. Look, I've been hitting the gym more, got a bit addicted. But I'm going to pull back," I lied.

He sniffed the air. "Fucking bullshit. You are tapping some sweet pussy and for some reason you're not telling me who it is."

"It's complicated," I told him, and he laughed.

"You should be a politician. Showing talent there for trying to part answer a question and get away with it." He slapped me on the back. "Fair enough, if you don't want to say. I'm sure you have your reasons."

He pointed from his eyes to mine with two digits. "But just know I'll be watching you. I'll make it my mission to find out what you're up to."

Fuck. That just made things a lot more difficult.

"I need to head up and get some studying done," I told him. "Got fucking behind. My dad is going to kill me if I start dropping grades."

"Well, less time studying pussy and more studying textbooks." He winked. "By the way, we're having a party here Tuesday night and I expect you to be there."

Tuesday. Fuck. That was the day I was going to see Meredith again. We were having tomorrow night off, which would make my head and balls explode. But I knew she was right, we'd got to rein things in and find some kind of happy medium between teaching and studying, and fucking each other raw.

"I'll be there, bro." We fist bumped. "I'll catch you later and I promise I'm going to be in my room more, around the lodge more. You gave me a great opportunity and I won't let you down, man."

Julian smiled. "We're going to have some fun, you and me. Before responsibility heads our way."

"Sure thing," I told him and as I went up to hit the books, I wondered what I was agreeing to.

Not seeing Meredith for two days almost killed me. We texted each other but it wasn't the same. It worked in so far as I got my course work caught up, but it was lonely in my own cold bed without Meredith's warm body held against my chest, my arms wrapped around her naked flesh. Plus, I was scared. Scared that if she spent time without me, she'd have second thoughts. That she'd decide it was all too much of a risk; that what she really needed was a man of her own age to settle down with. Just the thought of her even glancing in another guy's direction made my fists bunch. She was mine. We just had the next year to get through. Once I finished college, I'd be twenty years old and if we were still together—and I saw no reason why we wouldn't be—then I was in it for the whole caboodle: marriage, kids, everything.

The lodge was all worked up about the party and I still hadn't decided how I would work it out with seeing Meredith. Either I put her off until Wednesday or I snuck out of the party at some point to see her. In the end, I called her to let her decide.

"Hey, stranger," she answered.

"I know. It's tough not seeing you, but I know it has to be this way. We can't have you ruining your job and me failing my studies."

"I miss you though," she said softly.

"Me too," I admitted.

"I'm glad I'm seeing you tonight."

"About that..." I said, "The guys are having a party at the lodge. Julian's been giving me shit about not being around. He knows something's up, and he's threatening to follow me. I need to go to this, to put him off. He can't find out about us."

"Yeah, you should go then," she said. Her tone sounded sad, resigned.

"I can sneak out to you later tonight," I told her.

"No, stay at the party. It would only make Julian more suspicious if you disappeared. Do what you need to do to put him off the scent." There was an unspoken command in her voice.

"What do you mean, do what I need to do?"

She sighed. "Maybe you need to make out with someone your own age. Hell, maybe that's what you should do, anyway."

"Right," I huffed. "I'm coming over tonight as usual, while you're talking like this."

"No, Garrett. God, I'm sorry. Now I feel I'm pressuring you."

"I don't know what to do. We have another twelve months of this. Tell me what to do."

"Go to the party, Garrett, and I'll see you tomorrow night instead."

"You sure we're okay?" I checked.

"We are. Don't get too wasted though because Wednesday I will give you a workout. That'll be forty-eight hours I will have been without your cock. My pussy is going to be hungry."

"Well, I can see you tomorrow, or you can take another risk..." I teased.

"What risk?"

"You can sneak in to the party tonight. I'll sneak you past people and up to my room."

"That's crazy. We'd get caught," she said tersely. I imagined that was the voice her students got to hear when she was annoyed with them.

"You're right. We would," I told her. "Meet me at your classroom instead. I can sneak out for thirty minutes or so; you'll just have to make do with a quickie."

"I have a better idea," Mer said. "The tree I hid behind, at the back of the Dares Room. I want to fuck against it. It's dark there and behind it no one would see. Text me when it's dark and you're ready for me."

"I'm always ready for you," I told her, "But yes, I'll message you when it's dark."

The party was in full swing. There were huge punch bowls around the kitchen and living room that had God knows what in them. I stuck to beer, so I knew how much I was drinking. My roommates were drunk and loud and all had a girl on their arm. Julian brought a blonde over to me.

"This is Madelyn. She's yours for the night. You're welcome."

I looked at my watch. It was ten pm, and I was going to get Mer onto campus around midnight. I knew that to get Julian off my back I'd have to give this girl some of my time, so I asked what she wanted to drink and then hung out with her and my roommates. She was like a leech. She kept grabbing hold of my arm, wrapping her own around mine, like we were together. I wanted to smack her arm away, but Julian was watching me closely so instead I put up with it. The guys decided we should play spin the bottle just after eleven pm and Madelyn was all for it, leading me to the circle of other people and sitting at my side with her head resting on my chest. It all seemed so juvenile, and that was when I realized... I wanted no part of this. I'd grown up. What I wanted was to settle down, to have a family someday. This frat boy crap was not me.

So, much to everyone's surprise, including my own, I stood up, Madelyn's heading lifting in confusion.

"I'm out of here, guys. Have fun."

I went up to my room and closed the door on the lot of it.

Twenty minutes later there was a banging on my door. Sighing, I walked over and opened it to find Julian on the other side.

"What the fuck you doing, man? Have you forgotten how to have fun?"

"No." I shook my head. "I've just grown up."

A drunk Julian was no fun. His eyes steeled and his jaw set taut. "You've been no fucking fun since you moved in. I put my ass on the line to get you a place here, thinking we'd have some fantastic partying ahead, but it's like being roommates with a fucking boring nun. What is your problem, man? Can you not get it up or something? Madelyn is sweet pussy, and she already told me she would put out for you. Don't you want that? Are you like gay or something? Because that's fine, I can find you some cock to play with."

I pushed him to get him out of the door so I could close it again.

"Go back to the party, dude. I'm not gay, or a nun. Fuck, man, I just don't want to party tonight. I have other, better plans."

"Oh, so that's it, is it?" Julian sneered. "You think

you're fucking better than us. Well, you have a week to vacate this room. You're not staying here if you're too good to party with us."

I put my hands up. "Fine. I'll move. I only just moved in, but I'll move the hell back out. When are you going to grow up, Julian? You had all that shit at Lincoln High with Candy, and you're still getting drunk out of your head and acting like you have beef with everyone. The alcohol gives you issues, dude, and the sooner you realize that the better."

"The only thing, I realizzze," Julian slurred, "Is that everyone has a fucking opinion on my life and what I should do with it, and they should all just back off and mind their own goddamn business. Now I'm going back to the party to enjoy myself and score a prime piece of ass. For the last time, you coming?"

"No." I crossed my arms across my chest.

"Fuck you, Garrett." He staggered off back in the direction of the whooping and hollering coming from downstairs.

After that I didn't feel like getting Mer up here. I wasn't in the mood to be playing games behind trees. I just wanted her in my arms.

Garrett: Change of plans. I'm getting a cab to yours.

. . .

Mer: Everything okay?

Garrett: Yeah. See you soon.

When Mer opened the door to me, her face was a picture of concern. "What's wrong?" she said.

"I can't deal with it, Mer. The party tonight. My roommates were all like adolescents who had discovered their dicks for the first time. Getting wasted, playing juvenile games like spin the bottle and truth or dare, messing girls around hoping for some action. I know we were going to do the tree thing, but I needed out of there."

She smiled. "It's not like a desperate desire that we fuck behind a tree. We can do that some other time." She took my jacket from me. "You fancy a beer, or have you had enough to drink?"

"No, a beer would be great," I answered.

We snuggled up close on the couch watching tv. We weren't rushing to get each other's clothes off. Mer had read me correctly that I needed to chill after the party debacle. I enjoyed drinking my beer, curling up with my woman. That was all I needed in life, not the shit from Granger Lodge.

"Julian is kicking me out of my room," I told her. "Apparently I'm no fun."

Mer turned to me. "Which shows that he doesn't know you at all because I think you're a lot of fun."

"I'll have to see if I can get back into some student accommodation on campus. I'm going to look a whole heap of dumb at student services tomorrow when I only just moved out a month ago."

"Maybe he'll cool off when the alcohol wears off," she replied. "If you're stuck for a few days, you can stay here." Her body stiffened. "No pressure. You don't have to, and it could only be for a couple days."

I pulled her in close and kissed the top of her head. "Thank you. And I know I couldn't stay here long term. It is too risky. One year, Mer. One year and we can do what the hell we like."

"It's so long," she moaned.

"It'll pass quickly." I nibbled her earlobe. "I know things we can do to make the time pass even faster."

Meredith relaxed back against the couch and I placed our drinks down and moved over her body, capturing her lips with my own. We were both fully dressed, and we made out for ages: kissing, nibbling, stroking. No risky, forbidden fucking; just savoring each other and enjoying being close.

Mer began to rub her jeans clad core against my leg.

I pushed back on my arms and gazed down at her. "You want to move this to the bedroom?" I asked, raising a brow and looking at the bed just a short distance away.

"No, I'm okay here, if you are," she replied. "I never fucked on my couch before."

That was all she needed to tell me. The thought of claiming her, owning her in a place where no man had fucked her before, made my cock instantly erect.

Pulling her tee over her head I cast it to the floor and then shucked off her jeans, leaving her in just her underwear. I was in no rush. I stood and removed my own clothes, except for my briefs and then I moved us so her body was laid on top of my own. I crushed my lips to hers. My tongue entered her mouth, dancing with hers languidly. After a time, I flipped her over and trailed my mouth and tongue down her neck, feeling her shiver as I did so. I moved down to her breasts, unhooking her bra from behind and releasing the creamy orbs. Her nipples pebbled as I grazed my teeth over them in turn, alternating with soft taps to her swollen buds and pressing them between my fingers and rubbing. Her body undulated below mine as she became more turned on.

"Please, Garrett, make me come," she begged.

"All in good time," I replied.

Slowly, I trailed my lips over every part of her body, my teeth scraping against her skin slightly when I returned to her neck, or when I was at the juncture of her thighs. I lowered myself down to her feet and ran kisses up each leg in turn, teasing her by reaching the tops of her thighs and then starting again from the bottom of each leg. Her breasts were engorged stiff peaks. She was putty in my hands, looking at me with hooded eyes, filled with desire. Eventually, I ran my fingers over the top of the material of her panties. They were soaking wet, a damp patch visible. I pulled her panties down, lifting her butt up to do so. Then her plump pink lips were before me, and I spread them apart with my fingers and delved into her hot center with my tongue.

"Ohhhh."

The wait had meant that Mer was so sensitive; every lick, every graze over her core, drove her to distraction. She could hardly bear for me to continue. I continued to tease, light pressure making her rock and tilt her hips at me desperately as she sought her climax. I left her on the brink and returned right back to her mouth, letting her taste herself and then starting the descent down her body again.

"Garrett, what are you doing to me?" She sighed, her body and mind absorbed with desire. I took a moment to stare at the woman below me. At the faraway look in her eyes. At her enjoyment of what we were doing and her trust in me. I thought about what a far cry it was from what was no doubt happening right now at the lodge: quick fucks in bedrooms by drunken fools. It was night and day.

I pushed a finger into her core, curling it slightly. I could feel her honey running down my hand. She was so wet for me. Her eyes were now closed, and her eyelids fluttered as I teased her clit, rubbing and flicking the bud. Mer's cheeks were flushed and her breathing short and ragged, her breasts rising and falling in time with her breathing. I couldn't get enough of looking at her glorious body. The one that was all mine and waiting for me to claim her. I shed my boxers and hovered over my woman, lining myself up with her entrance and rubbing my cock backward and forward through the pool of her cream. Then I entered her leisurely, just the tip of my cock at first. I felt her try to raise her hips, to get me to sink further inside her, but I pulled my hips back so she couldn't do it.

"Garrett," she mewled.

I inched gently into her, keeping my leisurely pace until she was full of me and then I rocked in and out of her. She clung to me, her hands gripping my buttocks as I thrust inside her. I caught a pert nipple between my teeth and nipped there while I moved, and Mer sighed happily. Finally, when I decided I'd teased us enough, I slipped my hands under her buttocks so I could bring her closer to me. Keeping my speed languid, I increased the pressure, thrusting inside her to the hilt. With every thrust I pinched her clit. Mer's hips rose as if her pussy was trying to devour my cock. Her hips twisting from side to side as well as upward as she sought her orgasm.

"Oh my god, oh my god, oh my god," she cried as I encircled her clit with my finger and brought her to the brink. I felt her body begin to tense under me and then she exploded, wave after wave of her climax shuddering around my cock. Then she took me with her as my balls pulled back and I released my hot sticky cum inside her. I pulsed within her over and over, my come rocking me in its intensity. I stayed inside her while I adjusted our position, so we were side by side on the couch. She looked up at me, her eyes filled with something I could only hope I was right in defining.

"Mer, I love you," I told her and hoped to God, I hadn't just made the biggest mistake of my life and misjudged her emotions entirely.

CHAPTER TWELVE

Meredith

I'd had second thoughts about the whole fucking against the tree scenario, largely due to the high possibility of us being caught. I realized I preferred fantasy role play to actually taking chances. Pretending was just as hot when I was with Garrett.

I realized I had a stupid goofy smile on my face. Oh shit, I was really falling for the guy.

My heart warred with my head.

He was nineteen. I should let him be young and youthful, and end things. Let him sow his wild oats with those cute college girls he was partying with right then. I wondered how many were hitting on him.

Whether he was flirting back. Whether he felt he was making a mistake with me.

What the hell was I doing?

Then his text had arrived and sent me into a panic. Was he coming over to end things? Had he realized from being around his peers that this was crazy? He said everything was okay, but I hadn't believed him.

Not until he'd arrived and told me exactly what I'd wanted to hear—that he found his peers juvenile and he wanted to be with me. My heart had soared.

And then we had slowly made love. It was intense, and I reached heights I'd never reached before. He seemed to know exactly how to read my body and tune it to a mutual frequency.

I'd looked at him after I'd reached my climax and thought about how beautiful this man was. After which he'd told me he loved me.

Thoughts swirled around my brain in a vortex.

He loves me?
We just fucked.
Is that why he said it? Was he on a sex high?
He's nineteen.
I'm twenty-five.
He loves me?
I think I love him back.
Fuck.
I love him back.

Oh, he's staring at me. Now he's moving away.

"I'm sorry, Mer. You're not ready. I shouldn't have blurted it out like that. It's too early."

"No. No." I shook my head at him and clutched his bicep. "It's not. You just took me by surprise is all."

I grabbed his chin with my fingers and turned his face to look at me.

"Garrett, I love you too." I laughed. "This is crazy. I have known you like two minutes."

"I feel the same." He smiled. "Maybe what we feel is lust, not love, but I don't think so. It feels like love to me."

"Tell me again," I commanded.

"I love you," he said without hesitation.

"I love you too," I told him. My adrenaline was pumping, and I was ready for action all over again. I reached over and wrapped my hand around his dick.

"And I love your cock."

"I love you holding my cock."

I put him in my mouth and he pushed his hips toward me. "And I love you mouthing my cock," he added with a groan as I sucked hard.

When Garrett returned to the lodge the next morning, he called to tell me Julian didn't even seem to remember that he'd told him to move out.

"He just said, 'Hey, man, did you get some pussy,'" he told me.

"And I hope you told him the truth." I laughed.

"I did. I said I scored some real, hot pussy with an older chick."

"And what did he say to that?"

"He high-fived me."

I sighed, "So I guess tonight you need to stay at the lodge?"

"Yeah, I've offered to help tidy up. The place looks like the house was ransacked."

"Okay, well, I'll miss you, but I'll see you tomorrow."

"I could pop by your classroom after college…"

"You could…"

I spent my lunch with Tana who once again spoke about morning sickness and all the foodstuffs she couldn't eat. She made me feel guilty for tucking into my pastrami on rye, but I'd been working up quite an appetite these last few days and needed the calories.

"So how are things with you?" she finally asked. "Anything happening in your love life?"

"Nope," I told her, wiping my mouth with a napkin.

"Your face has pinked up. I know when you're lying; I lived with you long enough. Your face used to turn the same color when I would ask if you knew why my Jo Malone Orange Blossom bath oil had gone down. How did your date go with that PT? Anything I should know?"

"There's nothing to tell." I took another bite of my sandwich.

"You mean you won't tell me. I thought we were bff's and told each other everything?"

It'd been a long time since I'd considered us best friends. Her husband had come along and I was barely given a thought. I didn't say that to her face though. We had an amicable friendship, and I wanted to keep it that way. If she ever asked me to babysit though I'd be telling her to 'bite me.'

"Is he married? Is that why you're being all secretive?"

"No." I decided to offer her something to shut her up. "He's a couple of years younger than me that's all. I feel a little embarrassed about it."

"You're going to tell me he's all buff, aren't you? I

get it, you're going to marry him and have babies who grow up to enter the Olympics."

"You are so crazy, lady. We're just having fun is all. Lots and lots of..." I emphasized the word, "fun."

"I'm so jealous," Tana replied. "I'm too sick to move around having passionate, frantic sex."

"Yeah, well that's what got you in this trouble in the first place. I don't know about lately, but you and Don certainly had your moments. I used to have to turn my music way up high."

Tana sighed. "Those were the days."

"You sound like you miss them?"

"I kind of do. Don't get me wrong, I love Don and we are so excited for the baby, but you don't have that crazy newness you get with brand new relationships. It's different, and it's a good different, but I wonder when we'll get time to stay in bed for three days just sending for pizza in between fucking again."

I decided that was exactly what me and Garrett would do the weekend coming. Friday night until Sunday afternoon, bed and takeout.

"So, how long have you two been together?"

"A month. It's very new."

"But you like him a lot?" Tana queried. "I can see it in your expression."

"I really do," I told her.

Lunch drew to a close, and I promised Tana I

would keep her updated. I would need to get her onto a new baby obsession, like names or what color the nursery was going to be, anything to distract her from my love life. The afternoon was spent teaching class while I looked forward to the end of the day.

I had stayed in the classroom marking while I waited for nearby colleagues and other students to go home. When the coast was clear, I sent Garrett a text to let him know.

The classroom door opened, and he walked inside. I couldn't help myself, a massive beam of a smile lit up my face and I saw it mirrored in his own expression. He swaggered toward me, his super-hot body closing in on mine, and those muscled arms wrapped around my body folding me within. He may have been younger, but when we were together, I felt like the young one, in the protection of an alpha male.

"God, I miss you when we're not together," he told me. "Days seem to go on forever."

"Plus, hot sex with your cougar is much more fun than cleaning up empty bottles and vomit." I winked, looking up at him.

"Ugh, don't remind me. That's the joy I shall be returning to, so in this brief interlude, I think you should distract me."

Pulling him toward a chair, I lowered his pants and boxer briefs, and I took his cock in my hand, pumping it until he was hard and ready. I got him to sit on the chair and then I knelt at his feet, taking that huge cock into my mouth. Hell, I couldn't get enough of him: in my mouth, in my pussy, in my ass. I craved him so damn much. Sucking him until he came down my throat was such a turn on. I could watch his face, his eyes closing as I tongued his dick, could feel his climax approaching. He thrust into my mouth while groans emitted from his own.

"Mer? Are you still here? Only I'm feeling faint. Can you—"

We sprang back from each other, and the chair scraped against the floor. I wiped across my mouth while Garrett hurriedly put his cock back in his trousers. Then I turned to see the disbelieving face of Tana.

She grabbed the trashcan and threw up in it.

"Garrett, go home," I told him.

His bulky form towered over me. "No. I'm not ashamed. I'm staying here."

I touched his arm. "She's my friend, Garrett, please, and the pregnancy is really taking its toll. I don't want to put any extra stress on her. I will call you. Please, Garrett..." I looked at him with a pained stare.

"Okay." His cheek pulsed in anger. "I will expect a call from you, very soon, telling me she's okay and there's no problem here." He stalked away out of the classroom, his posture stiff and muscles rigid. The door banged behind him.

I passed Tana my bottle of water from the desk so she could swill out her mouth.

"You okay?" I asked her.

She swilled out her mouth, spitting it into the can and I took the can from her hands and carried it to the door, leaving it just outside. The smell was like nothing I'd ever smelled in my life.

"I saw your light was still on and I felt sick. I was just gonna rest here a minute." She shook her head. "Fuck, Meredith, a student? You said you met him at the gym."

"I did, and I had no idea he was a student until it was too late."

"It's wrong, Mer. You're years older than him. Not only is it against the college rules, but it's like you're taking advantage of a young student."

"It's not like that." I bristled. "We're in love."

She turned to me, her face all screwed up. "You're in love with a kid? What's his mother going to say about that do you think when she finds out? You'll lose your job, your pride, and your self-esteem. It'll be lust. God, I bet he's a rampant ride. But when you take away the sex, Mer, what's left? He'll want to sow his wild oats and you'll want to have kids soon. It's what you always said to me. Kids no later than twenty-seven, you hoped, so you could have two by age thirty."

I pulled up a chair at the side of her.

"It's not like that. I think he's my one."

She snorted with laughter at that. "You've been together a month, and no doubt been fucking like rabbits. You are in lust, Meredith, not love." She shook her head. "I can't condone this, Mer. It's against the rules for a reason. You're in a position of authority over this student."

"I don't teach him. If anything, he's teaching me!" I almost yelled. "I'm finding out who I really am, what I want from a relationship."

"It's coercion. Now I'm going to be a mom I see things from a different side."

I lost my temper at that remark. "Oh my god, you act like you're the first person ever to have a baby. You used to fuck anywhere you could for kicks but now you're going to be a mother you've gone all holier than thou."

She stood up, hands on her hips. "I don't recognize you right now, Meredith."

I stared up at her, "Yeah, well I don't know where Tana White went. She sure hasn't been around for a while."

"Tana White went when she got married and became Tana Geller and then got pregnant. I'm a grown up. You're the one acting like a spoiled brat of a child." She stormed toward the door. "Anyway, you end it, or I report you. It's as simple as that."

"And if I don't?" I challenged.

"Think about your boyfriend's future if you tarnish his reputation and he's ejected from his course. How will that go down with his parents? Think they are going to welcome you with open arms then?"

She stormed out of the room. The minute she'd gone I collapsed to the floor, tears falling and turning into wrenching great sobs.

What the hell was I going to do?

I texted Garrett and lied.

Mer: Tana's gone. She was shocked but is fine now.

Garrett: You need me to come back to the classroom?

Mer: No. I'm on my way home now. It's been a shock, but I'm fine.

. . .

Garrett: You sure? I'll ditch the guys and come over?

Mer: No. Take your part in clean-up. I just want an early night after what happened.

Garrett: She upset you?

Mer: We shocked/upset each other but all good now. We've been friends for a long time.

Garrett: Will she keep our secret?

Mer: Yes, it's all okay.

Garrett: Great. I'll see you tomorrow and we'll pick back up where we left off.

. . .

Mer: Can't wait.

But it was all lies. I was still upset. Tana and I weren't okay. She wasn't going to keep my secret and we couldn't pick back up where we left off. The more I thought about what Tana had said, the more I saw it from her point of view. What must have entered her mind when she walked in and found me on my knees with a student's cock in my mouth? I'd gone too far. I'd been taking risks at being caught participating in inappropriate behavior since my times with Marcus and it was time to face up to what I'd been doing.

My decision was made.

It was for the best that I left. Went somewhere else and started afresh. I had no ties to New York. Just old friendships which would never be the same after the harsh words that had been spilled. Both Tana's and my own lives had moved in different directions. We were no longer friends. It was time to move on.

I couldn't stand in the way of Garrett's career. He was all set for a position in the family business. His grades had been dropping because of all the time we were spending together. Plus, he needed a relationship with someone his own age. Tana was right—no matter how much I hated that she was—I was ready for someone to settle down and have babies with. Garrett was at the beginning of intimate relationships. He needed time to see what he wanted in life. To get his career started and see where life took him. I really would be a weight dragging him down.

Dragging a case out from underneath my bed and a large backpack, I began to pack my belongings into them. I didn't have much, it was mainly clothing I needed to take. Toiletries could be repurchased, so other than some travel-sized items and a toothbrush, I emptied everything else into refuse sacks. I loaded up my car with everything that needed to come with me and then I took out a map, decided on a new location and drove. Garrett would be furious I knew. He would text me and demand to find me, but I had to stay strong. He was better off without me. I would start afresh someplace else and date men my own age, looking for the guy I could settle down with. I ignored the voice in my head that kept trying to tell me that I'd already found him.

CHAPTER THIRTEEN

Garrett

I'd sent a text that night telling Meredith I loved her and she'd sent one straight back that said, 'I love you too.' That was the last I'd heard from her. There had been no answer this morning to any of my texts and I just knew something was off. My gut feeling told me that she was ending things, that Professor Geller had gotten to her.

I couldn't ask anyone. We had been informed that Professor Geller was on sick leave, with no planned date of return. That she probably wouldn't be back until after the birth of her baby. One student talked about a really bad morning sickness condition that often ended up in hospitalization, the student's sister had had it, so they speculated that was why she couldn't return.

It had given me no one to ask that day.

That evening when I'd still had no response or contact from Meredith, I traveled to her apartment. When I got there, I saw a cleaning crew.

"Do you know where the tenant went? Is she okay? She was a friend," I asked, desperation evident in my tone.

A guy walked out from the bathroom. "She went last night. Gave me no notice. Just gone." His hands gesticulated wildly. "She will get no deposit back. You know where she went?"

I shook my head, becoming angry. "Do you think I'd be here asking about her if I knew where she was? Do you have a forwarding address for her?"

"She left nothing. I told you that already."

"Screw you." I stomped down the hallway and out into the fresh air where I punched a nearby tree. My fist stung like fuck, but the pain was welcome, helping to ground my frustration. I knew what I needed right then. I needed to go to the gym, to take my anger out on the equipment while I thought of my next steps.

But there were no next steps.

Student services wouldn't give out personal details. They wouldn't mail a letter on.

The gym wouldn't tell me if they had any contact details for her.

Meredith changed her cell phone number.

It took a couple weeks of no contact before I finally realized that we were done. So, I did the only thing I could think of. I studied hard to get the best grades I could, I hit the gym hard to make sure my body was in peak condition, and I partied and fucked hard to try to forget Meredith Butler.

CHAPTER FOURTEEN

Meredith

I settled in Newport, Rhode Island. With its coastal scenery and beaches, it was a far cry from the moving and shaking of New York. I found a position as an accountant and rented a bedroom and bathroom in a colonial. The house was beautiful with luxurious interiors, and I had three roommates who had become great friends. I was mainly happy. I'd been dating and had had one semi-serious relationship. It'd had the potential to go all the way, but for one problem—I couldn't get Garrett out of my mind.

Every day I thought about him.

I wondered if he'd passed his course.

Settled in his job.

Moved on with someone else.

For all my plans to leave him behind, now a year had passed and all I could think was—had I made a mistake? I asked God for a sign and carried on with my life.

My boss was cursing about our computer systems.

"There has got to be a better way of doing this, Meredith. There has gotta be."

I looked up at him. "I knew someone whose family looked at systems for a living. Maybe you could give them a call?"

"Find me their number, would you? This needs sorting and fast. Time is money."

As I tried to Google Garrett's family business, I hid a wry smile. The pace of life here was so different from New York. My boss, Jack, would have had a heart attack working in the city.

I passed my boss the number and let fate decide if they could help Jack, and if they could, who would come to look at our systems.

Garrett

"I don't want to travel to Rhode Island. Tonight I have a hot date." I told my dad.

"Cancel it. Family comes first, son," he quipped.

"This is business, not family," I protested.

"It's a family business," Dad retorted.

I'd been working here for a few months now and my dad liked to send me on any jobs where there was a little more travel involved. He said I needed to expand my horizons. He didn't condone my one night only behavior with women and it had become a bone of contention, with him pulling me to one side last week and telling me I'd been raised better than that and to look for a woman I might settle with awhile.

I didn't tell him I'd done that. I'd found the woman for me.

That she'd left me broken for anyone else.

I couldn't do relationships. My heart still belonged to her, and I was scared it would do until it no longer beat.

I went home and packed a duffle bag with some belongings in case I had to stay over to get the job done, and then I said goodbye to my pops and took to the road.

It was only just over an hour's drive from Boston to Rhode Island and if I got the job done quick I could get back for my date with a blonde chick I'd chatted up in a diner the day before.

I arrived, found somewhere to relieve my bladder and grab some lunch, and then I made my way over to the accountants. I hated wearing a suit, but that was how my father insisted I dress, with me looking the part. Loosening my tie, I walked toward the door, knocking and then walking inside.

I heard a gasp, followed by the words. "Hello, Garrett."

My eyes fixed on the owner of a voice I would know anywhere. It haunted my dreams.

"Meredith? What the fuck is going on?"

Meredith

I spotted him walking toward the doorway. They'd told Jack to expect Mr. Garrett James by midday and here he was twenty minutes early. I'd never seen him in a suit. He looked so handsome, but so awkward. I'd watched as he'd pulled at his shirt collar as if it were strangling that corded, thick neck. He'd always looked mature for his age, but in his suit he looked every bit the mature businessman. I wanted to throw myself at his feet and beg for forgiveness, but I couldn't. Not right now at least. He was here to do a job.

"Meredith. What the fuck is going on?"

His steely blue gaze landed on me.

"You'd better take a seat. I'll grab you some water and explain."

I told him about the computers, that we needed a new streamlined approach, and that I'd thought of his father's business.

"That is not what I meant by what's going on and you know it."

"Not here," I said quietly. "After work. Maybe you'd come out for dinner with me. At least let me explain."

"You can damn bet I'll be coming out for dinner and your explanation better be a good one," Garrett fired at me. "Now let me look at these damn computers. If I can concentrate while you're around."

Garrett

Of course, you couldn't go to Newport without eating seafood on Newport harbor. We ordered a platter to share and a bottle of wine said to complement the tastes from the sea. And there over dinner Meredith informed me how she'd left so that I could pass my course and start my career.

"Well, you should have talked to me about that before you ran. In choosing not to do so, you treated me like the kid your friend was accusing you of seducing. You just bought right into what she was saying. It angered me that you didn't fight for us, Mer. You ran."

Meredith hung her head, and tears glistened at the bottom of her eyes.

"I know," she said softly. "And I've regretted it ever since."

"Have there been other men, after me?" I had to know.

She nodded her head, and it almost destroyed me. "Yes. A couple. But they were never you. Not even close. You?"

"I did what you wanted me to do, Mer. I fucked my way around and got it out of my system."

She took a sip of her wine. "I guess I deserved that."

I relented with wanting to hurt her. We'd wasted enough time. "They were never you. I never wanted to take things further because I'd already found the woman I wanted to spend the rest of my life with." I paused. "I just didn't know where she was."

"Garrett, I should never have listened to Tana. I

was a fool. Though I like Rhode Island. I don't regret moving from Brooklyn. This place is beautiful. It feeds my soul."

I looked around me. "It looks a great place. You chose well. I saw her, you know? Tana."

Her gaze flicked up toward mine again. "You did? When?"

"A couple of months ago," I told her, and I recounted the conversation I'd had with her friend.

There she was ahead of me pushing a pram and smiling into it like the cat that got the cream. That was until she saw my face, saw that she was walking toward me. Her face showed she recognized me instantly.

"Prof. Geller," I said. "It would seem congratulations are in order." I looked into the pram.

"Lia," she told me.

"You must be very happy," I replied.

"Yes, she's perfect." That smile at her daughter came again.

"It must be nice. To have that. A loving husband and a baby. Whereas because of you I don't have that happiness."

She flinched and looked around her, looking for potential escape routes if this got out of hand.

"Meredith left. I don't know if you ever found that out because you were sick, but she just upped and left.

No forwarding address. I have no idea where she lives or even if she's okay. I would have married her. We could have been having our own family now, but you made her feel ashamed of what we had."

"She was screwing a student. It was against the rules." Judgment clouded Tana's features.

"You never broke any rules? Never screwed your husband somewhere you shouldn't? Streamed a movie illegally? I was over the age of consent. The worst we did was screw in the classroom. That was stupid. We were carried away with lust, but we loved each other and because of you, now I'm unhappy, have been ever since she left." I paused for a moment. "Anyhow, when you go home tonight, take a good look at what you have around you and feel very grateful for it, because other people's actions can take it away, just like that." I snapped my fingers.

Her eyes narrowed. "Is that a threat?"

"No." I sighed. "I'm sorry if it came out that way. I'm just saying that when your daughter grows up and maybe she meets a guy who doesn't fit your perfect standards, cut her some slack, or you might just ruin her life, like you ruined mine." With that, I turned and walked away.

"Wow," Mer stated.

"Yeah. She called me back as I walked away. Said

for what it was worth she was sorry, and she hoped that maybe someday I would find you again. I just turned away from her and carried on walking. I wasn't only angry with her. She might have lit the stick of dynamite that blew us apart, but you were the one who let it explode."

"I made a mistake, Garrett." Those brown eyes fixed on mine, her gaze determined. "Now we can sit here, order a dessert, and continue to punish each other for it; or we can get the check, go to my room and start living the rest of our lives. It's up to you."

I got the check.

CHAPTER FIFTEEN

Meredith

I was so goddamn pleased he got the check.

We hurried back to my room and once through the door, clothes were shed like they were aflame. We kissed and nipped at each other's bodies as we shucked off our clothes and fell back onto my bed. It was like we wanted to devour each other. I couldn't stop running my hands over the grooves of his body, feeling the sinews of his still toned arms, the smoothness of that taut, ripped abdomen. Our bodies remembered each other's instantly and clamored to make up for all that lost time. Juices pooled between my thighs.

"I just need to be in you, Mer. I can't wait."

"Yes, do it. I feel the same."

Without hesitation, he took hold of his erect cock, lined it up at my entrance and thrust into me all the way home. We groaned and moaned in unison as our bodies made the most intimate connection. His thrusts were frenzied, and I bucked up to meet every one of them. Sweat poured down our faces, and we were breathless as frustration, anger, loss, and lust made themselves known.

We exploded, reaching our crescendos together.

The relief about now, or sadness about the time we had lost made tears course down my cheeks.

"Mer, no. No, no, no. Don't cry. I'm here, don't cry."

"I could have lost this forever. Damn, I was so stupid."

His fingers came under my chin and he tilted my face up to look into my eyes. "We have found each other again, Mer. No looking back, okay? No looking back, ever."

I nodded and his lips swept down, his tongue licking up every last drop of my tears and replacing them with brushes of loving kisses.

The kisses then trailed down my neck, down onto my chest, around my breasts, down across my stomach and then down each thigh one at a time, until he rested his head between my legs and his tongue darted out and licked my core, causing my hips to raise from the bed. God, I'd missed him. This second time we took all the time we needed. His tongue delved and teased, building me back up to ride yet another crest of a wave as I came against his mouth. He sucked in my juices greedily.

I moved us so he was sitting at the edge of my bed and I took him in my mouth. I don't know if he realized it—his eyes seemed to understand, as he looked at me, although they were filled with lust—that this was where we'd been, the exact position, all those years ago when I'd allowed Tana to drive me away. Right now, I had taken us back to that time, and I was holding on for dear life.

I took him to the back of my throat, sucking hard and caressing his balls with my fingers. Next, I moved him so he was back in my hand and I flicked my tongue around his tip and teased the underside of his cock. Then I took him back in my mouth increasing the strength of my sucks and I looked up at him while I did it. Watching him watching me. I hoped I looked like I was serving him, giving my all to the worship of his cock, and to him. His hands came around to hold the back of my head as his hips thrust upwards. He fucked my mouth hard, and I held fast until he came, his cock shuddering in my mouth as spurts of creamy, salty cum bathed my throat.

We moved up to my bed and got under the

comforter and Garrett held me in his arms while we dozed. It was all so familiar from what we'd enjoyed before, but I didn't know what would happen from now. I let sleep take me so I could face whatever happened next.

I stirred as I felt Garrett move away from me.

"Garrett?" I questioned, panicking that he was leaving me.

"Babe, I'm just going to your bathroom to freshen up. I'll be right back."

My heart beat fast as I collapsed back against my pillows, praying that he wouldn't leave me, like I had him.

Thankfully, he returned from the bathroom, pulled me into his arms and made sweet love to me all over again, until eventually we were so exhausted we slept.

When the morning came, I explained he might see my roommates downstairs.

"You made new friends, huh?"

"Yes, I did." I smiled. "I really needed some."

"It's good to have girlfriends," he said. "Just make

sure to let them know that you'll have less free time to spend with them now though."

"Oh yeah?" I asked him.

"Yeah. Because you're dating me now, Meredith Butler. Dating me exclusively." He ran a hand over his body. "And see this here? I'm a man. Don't let anyone tell you otherwise, babe. I don't give a crap about the age difference between us." He rolled me under him again and thrust his dick against my core once more. "Feel that? We fit together perfectly. You and me. That's how we roll. We're perfect."

And he proved that to me again.

By the time we made it down to breakfast, my roommates had gone.

"Ah, well, I'll meet them another time. Right now, I just want to eat you, not breakfast."

I went to the stove and cooked some bacon and eggs. "We need sustenance, Garrett. I'm ravenous. Then I need to get to work. I've never been late a day in my life and I'm not starting now." I winked at him. "Even if it would be worth my while."

We ate our breakfast, drank some coffee, and went into work where Garrett finished the job on the computers and got ready to drive back to Boston.

"So, when am I going to see you again, boyfriend?" I asked him. I tried not to show him, but I was nervous that once he drove home, he might never come back. It seemed too good to be true that he was back in my life, and part of me wondered if this was a plan of revenge where he would never return. Until he took me in his arms and kissed me and reassured me in that kiss that he was going nowhere.

"I'll be back tomorrow evening to take you to dinner again, Miss Butler. I fancy trying the lobster next time. Get dressed, ready for about eight pm, and I'll come call on you. We'll have a pleasant stroll hand in hand down to the harbor.

"I'll look forward to it," I said, and I kissed him hard and watched him leave.

"That guy must have done a really great job on the computers," quipped Jack.

The smile that broke across my face was huge.

CHAPTER SIXTEEN

Garrett

As promised, the next evening I returned and picked up my girl at eight. We had a booking at the restaurant for eight thirty, and so had time to take a lovely stroll together. I held her hand in mine the whole way. She was wearing the most beautiful red dress that ran close to her hips but then floated at knee length. All I could think of was getting my hands under it and into her panties, but we were eating food before I got to eat her.

They'd set us a table for two out front, looking out over the harbor. I could imagine you'd never get bored with this view.

Mer ordered a glass of wine and I chose to have a beer this time. It might not complement the food, but it would help settle my nerves. Meredith ordered a starter, so by the time the main arrived I could barely hold my glass. Thank God she'd not protested about me ordering the lobster. The waiter brought out a silver platter, and as he placed it on the table in front of us, I watched as Meredith's gaze fixed on the lobster's claw, which was holding a diamond engagement ring. A simple solitaire that glistened under the evening sunshine.

I dropped to my knees at the side of her. "Meredith Butler, would you do me the honor of becoming my wife?"

"Yes." She nodded. A tear forming at the corner of her eye. "Oh my god, yes, Garrett. Yes."

I took the ring and placed it on her finger. It was a little loose, but the jeweler had assured me that could be fixed, no problem.

"Could we have a bottle of champagne, please?" I asked the wait staff, who nodded and left to get some.

I toasted my future wife, and we enjoyed the rest of our meal. Mer kept staring down at the ring like she couldn't believe it was there, like she was dreaming or something.

"I'll move to Boston," she announced. "Garrett, I want to be wherever you are."

"I'm going to be right here, baby," I told her. "My work takes me all around here. I can set up an office here if I need to." I caught her hand in mine and stroked her fingers. "This place looks like a great place to bring up kids and I think we need to go house hunting and get one of those lovely colonials for ourselves. One with plenty of room for babies."

"You mean it? We can live here?"

"Seems perfect to me," I said. "Just like you are."

EPILOGUE

Meredith

"It's about time that boss of yours realized you were over eight months pregnant," Garrett scolded me as he watched me get ready to head to work.

"Oh, don't you start again. Jack is the same. Says if I ruin his carpets with my waters breaking, he's going to make me replace them."

"So why aren't you listening?"

"I love my job, Garrett, and you know my obstetrician has no problem with me continuing to work. Says I'm as fit as a flea."

He gathered me into his arms and kissed the top of my head.

"Now, you go too. Get off to work and I'll call you if anything happens."

"You're so damn bossy." He raised a brow at me. "Anyone would think you used to be a teacher."

He winked.

NEWPORT ECHO

Births and announcements

To Garrett and Meredith James
A son
Chance Miller James.
7lb 6oz
Born 26 September 2017.

THE END

Read on for news of three **FREE** Angel Devlin books.

Have you read **Rule Him**? Book one of the Forbidden Fantasies series?
Check it out here: https://books2read.com/u/bPyEjr

Note from the author.

Thank you so much for reading Teach Her. If you have time, I'd be very grateful if you could leave a review.

Angel xo

ANGEL DEVLIN FREE SERIES STARTERS

Fix My Heart – The Waite Brothers Book One
https://books2read.com/fixmyheart

Milo Waite is determined to fix her home, and her heart…

After Violet Blake buys her nan's former home, she's shocked to find it in a state of neglect. When the local renovation company come to assess the property, builder Milo makes it his mission to ensure Violet has a safe home to live in. But he has another mission too… to capture her heart. However buried family secrets threaten not only their budding relationship, but to tear their families apart. When the dust settles, can Milo and Violet have a happy ever after?

Fix My Heart is the first in a series of contemporary romances set in a fictional small town in the U.K.

Sold – Romance In NYC: Double Delight Book One

https://books2read.com/u/bwoPWO

I was always told things came in threes…

Everything changes for Realtor, Tiffany, with an anonymous email to her business account where the sender describes what he'd like to do to her in vivid detail.

Then she meets him at a viewing - H, owner of Club S, where patrons bid for the stage. Soon the email is being lived out in the flesh. After, H asks her the question, "Have you ever had two men at once?" Tiffany leaves.

With no further contact, Tiffany begins dating neighbour Brandon, but she can't get thoughts of H and threesomes out of her mind, especially after she visits the club and sees one up close.

She wonders if Brandon is going to be enough for her,

until a shock encounter means she doesn't have to wonder any more...

Hot Daddy Sauce – Hot Single Dads Book One

https://books2read.com/u/38dBed

Join Angel Devlin and Tracy Lorraine as they delight your mind with stories of single dads and happy ever afters!

Leah

My next door neighbor, Jenson, is a chef and a successful businessman. He's also a single daddy to the cutest six-year-old girl.

I'm only here as long as it takes to get my parents' old house ready for sale. Then it's time for me to make a fresh start, away from the tragic events of late.

Trouble is, now I've had a taste of this hot daddy's sauce, I want more...

Jenson

When I see Leah in the garden next door, at first I think she's barely out of school. But she soon reveals she's all woman.

My daughter loves her and it's not long before my own feelings are heading the same way.

Are we a mouth-watering combination or a recipe for disaster?

This is the first book in a complete series of interconnected standalones (each book can be read separately but some characters from previous books re-appear).

FREE STORY WITH NEWSLETTER SIGN UP

Did you know I have a newsletter? I love it because I can write to you with news of work-in-progress, sales, giveaways, and general updates about my life!
You also get a FREE short story, the prequel to Rats of Richstone, BAD BAD BEGINNINGS.
So sign up today. I look forward to connecting with you.
Angel xo

https://geni.us/angeldevlinnewsletter

ABOUT ANGEL

Angel Devlin writes stories about bad boys and billionaires. The hotter, the better.
She lives in Sheffield with her partner, son, and a gorgeous whippet called Bella.

When not working, she can be found either in the garden, drinking coffee, watching too much TikTok, or daydreaming about her ideal country cottage.

She's a firm believer in living in, and enjoying every moment and hopes her words bring you that enjoyment. Let her know by leaving a review, joining her newsletter, or dropping her a line via Facebook DM or email.

E-mail: contact@angeldevlinwriter.com

Printed in Great Britain
by Amazon